Tea Cozies
and
Terabytes:

People

Tea Cozies and Terabytes: People

By The WordWeavers

©2018 by WordWeavers, Bartlesville, OK

All rights reserved.

This book or parts thereof may not be reproduced in any form, stored in a retrieval system, or transmitted in any form by any means without prior written permission of the authors, except as provided by United States of America copyright law.

Cover/Interior Design: Brandy Walker
www.facebook.com/SisterSparrowDesign
Executive Editor/Format Design: Jennifer McMurrain

ISBN-13: 978-1729793398

The following is a work of fiction and nonfiction. Some names, characters, places, and incidents are fictitious or used fictitiously. Any resemblance to real persons, living or dead, to factual events or to businesses is coincidental and unintentional in stories of fiction. The views expressed in this works are solely those of the individual author.

Also available in eBook publication

PRINTED IN THE UNITED STATES OF AMERICA

A special thanks to each and every WordWeaver who participated, whether they submitted or just critiqued. This book would be nonexistent if not for your creative minds. Special thanks to Ann Cleary, Linda Derkez, and Olive Swan for copy editing. R. D. Sadok, Olive Swan, and Saralyn Miller for heading our cover design committee. Brandy Walker for our beautiful cover design. Glen Mason and Antoinette Yvette Mousseau heads of our BETA reading committee. Meredith Fraser and Jayleen Mayes our public relations committee and to Jennifer McMurrain for formatting and organizing the anthology. It takes a village to produce a book and we have a very special and talented village. Thank you everyone.

This book is dedicated to our writing friends: those who cheer us on, helps us with twists, and pick us up when things get hard. Writing might be a solitary process, but writing life is anything but.

Table of Contents

Finding Thanks   Marilyn Boone   4

When Snowflakes Fall   C. L. Collar   11

In the Event of …   Linda Derkez   15

Revoked   Linda Derkez   27

Friends Forever   Rita Durrett   39

Houdini   Rita Durrett   48

Butterfly Mims   Meredith Fraser   52

Rock Chalk Jayhawk KU   Pepper Hume   57

A Red Tri Aussie   Pepper Hume   66

Grace   Glen Mason   77

Old Doctor Palmer   Glen Mason   79

Love Me No Less   Glen Mason   82

The Trash Truck Comes at Nine   Glen Mason   84

Space Cowboy   Jayleen Mayes   86

Old Sight   Jennifer McMurrain   93

New Sight   Jennifer McMurrain   103

Show & Tell Daddy   Cindy Molder   114

Choice   Cindy Molder   120

Tea Cozies and Terabytes: People

Wednesday Morning   Eloise Peacock   124

Frank's Five Hundred MPH Mouse   R. D. Sadok   128

Awards Ceremony   R. D. Sadok   144

Forever Faithful   Olive Swan   156

Forever Family   Olive Swan   167

The Age of Silicon   Antoinette Yvette Mousseau   185

The Age of Iron   Antoinette Yvette Mousseau   191

Finding Thanks

Marilyn Boone

Lisa climbed up the old maple tree in the backyard and settled into her favorite spot. She needed to feel the sturdy trunk and the curve of the branches that held her as a pair of arms would, especially now. It seemed impossible for Thanksgiving to be the next day, but then again, nothing seemed as it should. She certainly never imagined she would become an orphan at the age of fifteen.

First, it was her father's death a few years earlier, and then her mother's in late October. Her brother, James, was four years older and barely old enough to be her legal guardian, but they convinced their mother that was what they wanted, what they thought was best. Lisa wasn't as sure anymore.

"It's time for us to leave."

Lisa looked down from her resting place into the stoic face that accompanied the stern voice. "You could say it a little nicer."

"All I know is I told Aunt Kay we would be there by 5:00 and it's already after 4:00. I'll be waiting in the car," he said, stopping long enough to add, "Aren't you too old to be climbing trees anyway?"

Lisa answered with a firm, "No," but only to herself. The tree was a part of her. They had grown up and changed seasons together. It had been a living space for her as much as it had been for the families of birds that built nests and made it their home.

A gust of wind wrapped a swirl of falling red leaves around her as she climbed back down, almost as if they were speaking to her. Lisa picked up one of the most crimson colored ones to keep, afraid the branches would be completely bare by the time they returned from their aunt and uncle's. She hurried on inside the house to grab her small suitcase and spend a moment petting Bishop, their golden retriever. Lisa was certain he sensed the changes in their lives as well.

After putting the suitcase in the back seat, Lisa slipped into the front. "I wish Bishop was going with us. It doesn't feel right leaving him alone for the holiday."

James started backing out of the driveway. "Aunt Kay and Uncle Bill don't allow dogs in the house. The Sanders will take good care of him."

Lisa didn't understand how he could sound so indifferent, like their entire world hadn't been turned upside down. "But what if they never forgave him for chasing that blue jay through their flowerbed of prized tulips?"

James shot her a frown. "Don't be ridiculous. That happened a long time ago when Bishop was just a puppy."

Lisa bit her bottom lip trying to contain her still fragile emotions. This would be her first Thanksgiving dinner away from home. As much as she loved her aunt and uncle, going there was just another painful reminder of how her life would never be the same.

Aunt Kay was on the front porch, waving to them as they pulled up. She gave James a hug first then let her arms linger around Lisa a little longer. "I've got a big pot of chili simmering on the stove. We'll eat as soon as your Uncle Bill finishes cleaning up. He got extra dirty working in the field today."

Lisa tried not to stare when her uncle eventually made his entrance into the kitchen. Every time she saw him she felt like she was seeing a ghost. While he and her father weren't twins, they almost looked like they could have been.

"How are my favorite niece and nephew?" he bellowed.

Lisa managed to crack a small smile as she began carrying bowls of chili to the table. "Uncle Bill, we are your only niece and nephew."

He gave her a wink as he sat down. "You'd be my favorite just the same."

As Lisa sat his bowl in front of him, she picked up a scent, different from the warm spices in the chili. It was immediately familiar, yet something she hadn't smelled in a long while.

"Is everything all right, Lisa?" Aunt Kay asked.

It was then Lisa realized her feet hadn't moved from beside her uncle. "Yes, I'm fine," she nodded and continued on around the table to her chair.

Lisa remained quiet throughout the rest of the meal, her thoughts having spun back to the last time she remembered playing dress up. She had opened a drawer next to the one containing her mother's make-up and found a bottle of perfume she hadn't seen before. The only rule was not to use the good perfume on top of the vanity. Lifting the bottle to her nose, Lisa decided to put some on. She would never forget how quickly her mother's smile faded when she then went out to model in front of her.

"Lisa, what perfume did you use?" her mother asked.

"It wasn't your good bottle, I promise," she answered, suddenly afraid she had done something wrong. "I'll show you."

Lisa ran back into her mother's room to retrieve the milk-colored bottle with the picture of a blue sailing ship on the front and brought it to her.

A wistful smile returned to her mother's face as she took the bottle and gave Lisa an assuring hug. "This is your father's old cologne. I thought I had given it to your Uncle Bill since they wore the same one."

The next time Lisa saw the bottle it was on her brother's dresser. She understood why her mother gave it to him, but that didn't keep her from sneaking into his room every chance she had. That's when she would pull off the cologne's top and close her eyes, taking deeps breaths each time to create a permanent memory of the scent.

Lisa discovered her eyes had drifted over to her uncle by the time she shook her thoughts back to the present and stood up to help clear the table. Aunt Kay was already rinsing dishes at the sink. "Can I do anything to help you get the turkey ready? Mom always wanted to make sure it was plenty thawed the night before."

Aunt Kay turned off the water and dried her hands. Her face wore a look of apology when she turned back around.

"I'm sorry, Lisa, I thought you knew I was allergic to turkey. That's why I always brought a ham when we came to your house."

The full meaning of her aunt's words took a minute for Lisa to process. Once they did, she felt her heart shatter a little more. There would be no turkey in the oven for her to baste tomorrow, one of the first jobs her mother had given her as a little girl.

"I'm not feeling very well," Lisa said, rushing out of the kitchen and up the stairs to the bedroom she was staying in. As soon as she closed the door, the tears burst onto her cheeks. She fell onto the bed, wanting desperately to go home and curl up next to Bishop. How could she be expected to eat a dinner she wasn't thankful for on Thanksgiving? How was she supposed to even celebrate Thanksgiving at all?

Lisa was still on the bed a short time later, when there was a knock on the door. She decided it was better not to answer than let her aunt see how awful she looked and feel worse for something that wasn't her fault.

There was a second knock, this time followed by, "May I come in?"

The voice wasn't Aunt Kay's, it was her brother's. Lisa heard the door crack open and knew she couldn't continue to ignore him. "Sure, if you want," she mumbled.

Lisa refused to face him as he entered the room, bracing herself for a lecture on how rude she was to run out of the kitchen and how ungrateful he thought she was behaving. The corner of the bed lowered as James sat down, but nothing was said.

When Lisa finally looked at him she saw a difference in his demeanor. Instead of the stiff posture he had been trying so hard to maintain, his shoulders were slumped and his head was lowered. He looked beaten, only without the cuts or bruises.

"I miss them as much as you do, Sis," he said softly.

Lisa pushed herself up. He hadn't called her that since before the funeral. "I know, but the way you've been acting has made me feel like I not only lost my parents, but I lost my brother, too."

James lifted his head and focused his gaze on her. "I'm scared. I don't know if I can handle being your guardian while going to school at the same time." He turned away to continue. "I've been thinking more and more that we should move in with Aunt Kay and Uncle Bill for a while."

"No," Lisa snapped, "That would mean Bishop would have to stay outside all the time."

The words had no sooner left her mouth when Lisa realized how selfish she sounded. Her brother had already made sacrifices, leaving the university he loved to transfer to the community college in town after their mother became ill. It was only fair she should have to make sacrifices as well.

She placed her hand on top of his. "I don't want to move out here, but I'll let it be your decision. All I need is for you to be my big brother again. You're the best one a sister could ask for," she added with a nudge.

The corners of his mouth softened. "What happens if I mess up?"

"You won't. And we'll always have Aunt Kay and Uncle Bill when we need them."

"How about when you start dating?"

Lisa smiled for the first time in weeks, having one boy in mind already. "Whoever it is will just have to meet your approval first."

James returned a smile and held out his hand, "Deal."

Lisa threw her arms around his neck instead. Whether or not they would be eating turkey for Thanksgiving didn't matter anymore. They had each other, and that was all she needed to be thankful.

When Snowflakes Fall

C. L. Collar

I open my door and step out into the dense night. The cold wind tosses my long dark hair into my eyes. As I look up toward heaven, large soft snowflakes mingle with salty droplets on my face. The cold from the storm is nowhere near as frigid as my feelings. My feelings that are now frozen in time. A snowflake falls on my palm. It's there for just a second and then it's gone. Just like you.

My mind reels back to the day of your skiing accident. Oh, how you loved to ski. I never liked the cold winter air, but you thrived in it. I remember sitting in the bar at the resort, sipping my hot spiced wine and waiting to see you come flying down that mountain, in blissful ignorance of the fact that you were instead flying to a hospital nearby.

When I think of how irresponsible that young snowboarder had been, I want to rip his head off. They say he was drunk and had been skiing recklessly all morning. He plowed right into you, sending both of you tumbling down the mountainside. You never knew what hit you. I want to scream at him, to hit him, to tear his heart out like he has torn mine. But I cannot release my anger on him because he also left this world that day.

Yesterday I drove up the slippery mountain road to our secret place, the place where our hearts merged into one. I hadn't been back there since we said our last goodbyes. I kept thinking the sight might bring some feeling back into my life. This numbness in my soul drives me crazy. I want to yell, scream, maybe even smile, but there is nothing left in my heart. It is empty.

Today I went to church. I asked God to help me understand. I asked him to take me too so that I could spend eternity with you. I received no reply. I knelt at his alter and cried until there were no more tears left.

Do you remember the night we walked hand in hand, commenting on how much brighter the stars looked after the first snow? We danced in the drifts and slid on the icy sidewalks. The warmth of your love kept the chill of the day at bay.

We were children again. Oh, how I wish we could go back to that day, that time. I wish to feel like a little girl again. I have to wonder, is there still a child left in my soul? Right now. I think not.

Swoosh. Smack.

"What the ...? Okay. Who threw the snowball? Where are you? Don't you know how childish that is?" I yell into the darkness, while digging the snow out of my neckline. "What is wrong with you? I see you hiding behind that tree. Come out now and explain yourself."

"I thought you wanted to play in the snow, just like a child again. Isn't that what you just said?"

A young man steps out from behind the tree. Snow covers his wavy blond hair. His light blue eyes twinkle in the soft light as an ornery grin spreads across his lips. Lips that had once touched mine so passionately.

"No. This can't be. You left me five days ago. You left me alone and broken." I back slowly away from the all too familiar voice and I turn to run from the pain, the hope.

"Don't go, Cassy. I only have a small amount of time here and I want to spend every moment with you before I have to go."

I stop in my tracks and turn, running as fast as I can straight into the arms of my love. "I have missed you so much, Tim. My heart hurts, it's torn apart. Please take me with you," I pleaded.

"Now Cassy, you know that isn't up to me. But because you went to that church today and asked God for help he let me come back to give you a message. He wants you to know that he needs me back in heaven. My work on earth is done. He seems to think I would make a perfect guardian angel, since I can't stay out of other people's business."

Tim chuckles into my hair as he holds me tight.

"This is not funny, Tim. I can't go on without you. How can you be so nonchalant about all of this?" I wave my hand out into the universe as I push myself away. "You're going to leave me all alone in this world. What am I supposed to do?"

"I'm not going to leave you. I'll be with you every day. That's the cool thing about being an angel. You can be in all places at one time. Give me one last kiss goodbye. After that I'll see you in your dreams."

I close my eyes as my body clings to his. I take in the feel of his full lips on mine, his smell, his whole being.

Then he pulls away and begins to fade.

"I have left something for you." I hear his soft whisper in my ear.

"What is it?"

"You'll know when the snowflakes fall."

"But Tim, they are falling now. Tim, Tim?

Bright lights sting my eyes. I hear a siren. It's close by. What's happening? Wait a minute. I'm floating. No, I'm being lifted onto a bed. The siren sounds are getting closer. I hear someone ask, "Why was she out in the storm in only her nightgown?"

Another voice, this one deeper, a man's. "She recently lost her husband. I would assume she is suffering from grief."

As my bed rolls toward the bright lights and loud sirens, I hear Tim's soft whisper in my ear. "Be careful with her, boys. She carries my child."

I smile as I slip into sweet oblivion and a tear escapes my eye. I place my hand on my stomach. "Thank you for such a precious gift, my love. Now I'll never be alone and I'll always have a part of you here with me. I look forward to seeing you in my dreams."

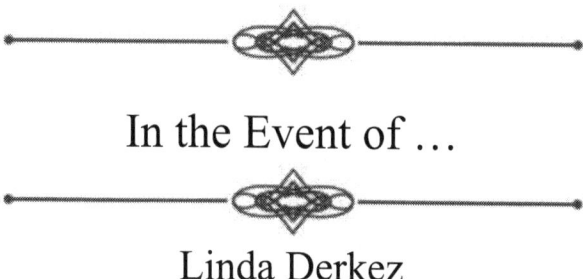

In the Event of ...

Linda Derkez

The multicolored squares of my bell-bottom pants dragged on the dewy grass of the campground, making the pattern even darker. I held my clogs in my left hand, preferring to be barefoot but also wanting my shoes to be dry when I put them back on. After watching an episode of *Super Friends*, my eleven-year-old sister Sue and I were imagining we were the Wonder Twins. She ran ahead of me, pretending to be an ocean wave in her stained Kool-Aid Man t-shirt and blue shorts with white trim. Her tube socks were pulled up tightly to just under her knees. Dad, always worried about money, would yell that she was wrecking the elastic.

"It would be far-out if you took the form of a snake," my sister (also known as the male Wonder Twin named Zan) said, looking back at me. Her red Kool-Aid mustache seemed to coordinate with her shirt. The funny thing was we hadn't had red Kool-Aid for days. Crossed over her shoulder was a faux suede purse covered in tiny beads. We both sported short shags cut by our mom, only mine was dirty blond and hers was brown. I told Mom I wanted my hair to look like Farrah Fawcett, but she just laughed and made me look more like David Cassidy than one of *Charlie's Angels*.

"Get real. I don't like snakes," I said, "they freak me out." The grass was long, and I started to imagine a snake hiding in the wet blades. I placed my next steps more deliberately.

"But a snake could climb into the trailer and look around,'" my sister pointed out, "and that would be cool."

I was the female Wonder Twin, Jayna, but my real name was Tammy. Maybe it was because I was a whole year younger, but, at ten, I always seemed to be the girl, and she was the boy when we acted out different people.

I stopped checking for grass snakes, stopped walking, and squinted to get a better look at the ominous, broken-down trailer house in the distance. We were spending our summer at a campground for my dad's job. All around were regular campers: big, small, old, new. Among them, as if it'd been thrown away, a trailer the size of a school bus sat abandoned. The curtains were drawn together like a lady caught in her nightgown trying to throw an old robe together around her middle. The trailer was white with a goldenrod stripe along the sides. Bits of things were tossed around the yard: an old grill, a chair without a seat, some cushion material with yellow insides spilling out like guts.

My bell-bottoms were bold, but I wasn't. My heart sped up the same way it did at those times when I had to go downstairs in the dark by myself to use the bathroom. "Maybe... Maybe we shouldn't go there," I said quietly.

"Don't be a spaz," my sister said, dismissing my fear. Suddenly, she stopped. She was bony so her legs were like two broomsticks in her black & white saddle shoes.

Uneasiness came like a warning. Sue's big eyes met mine. In that stare, I got the impression she was as delicate as a breakable vase—the kind that costs more money than a year's allowance, and you knew your mom would kill you if you broke it. A good vase, not a regular one, kept in the company-ready living room where kids weren't allowed. Where even the store covering stayed on the velvet lampshade and protective plastic covered the plaid couch. A sixth sense I didn't know I possessed whispered of the need for a protective covering over my sister.

The Oklahoma morning was warm and muggy, yet this Wisconsin girl shivered.

"I have to use the bathroom," I lied. That wasn't the reason. Sue knew I was lying and she knew I knew she knew I was lying.

"Get real, you fibber." Sue bent over to tug her red-ringed socks up. I thought I heard the elastic screaming for mercy. "You can't be a Wonder Twin if you're a 'fraidy cat."

"Can too," I said and thrust my fist toward her to mimic summoning my super-powers. "Wonder Twin powers: Activate. Make me the shape of a chicken."

My sister had the goofiest laugh--sometimes I thought it was specifically designed to make *me* laugh along with her--and she snorted before breaking into her hyena guffaw. Pretty soon my side hurt, and then I really did need the bathroom.

"Come on," Sue said, nodding toward the haunted trailer. "Let's get crackin', Chicken."

* * *

Someone had neglected to lock the door. The screen door hung there like a loose tooth in need of one brave pull.

I slipped into my clogs, not knowing if it was with the purpose to walk inside or to walk away. My sister's reassuring look helped me to step up the rickety wooden staircase on the way to the belly of the trailer.

Sometimes I was smart--not often--but this was one of the times. Planning to trick her into going into the scary place first, I practically tripped over myself to hold open the already mostly open screen door. "After you," I said grandly, as if Sue qualified as royalty.

My sister looked at me in a way that promised revenge at the first chance if our little adventure went awry. She rolled her big eyes and sighed at the injustice while bowing to my ingenuity. Sue reached for the doorknob.

The smell hit us first, damp and old and stale. To my vivid imagination, it was as if the door was the trailer's mouth and, when it opened, warm, mildewy breath blew in our faces. Somewhere in the back of that unpleasant scent lingered a hint of gasoline, a smell I associated with my dad's garage.

I wanted to be brave and spy-like, but in reality, I was ready to go home. If not for my sister, I would have gone home to more cartoons and maybe another bowl of Buc Wheats cereal.

It was the story of my life: wanting to do one thing but doing the opposite instead for a reason I couldn't even define. I wanted to be a grownup and have my own *Brady Bunch* house where I wouldn't have to clean my room (Alice would clean it for me). I wanted to be free and drive around in a black Trans Am wherever I wanted to go instead of facing backward in my parents' station wagon. I wanted to be thought of as a person all on my own, not just an extension of my sister. To the people around us, we were "the girls" whether we were together or apart. To my parents, one comic book or *Tiger Beat* magazine, and one candy bar or soda pop or gift of any kind was to be shared, as if we were two parts of one whole. I refused to dress alike; that was about all I could do to rebel.

Yet all the while I copied whatever Sue did, thought like she thought and followed her whole-heartedly, letting her lead me because I couldn't make any decisions on my own or come up with an original thought.

As much as I wanted freedom and lone-dog independence, really I was little more than a tag-along pooch, hot on Sue's heels when she was outside or nestled next to her lap on the couch when she was inside.

I didn't resist now as, without a word, somehow knowing how scared I was, she took my hand and drew me further inside the eerily quiet trailer. I looked at her hand joined with mine and concentrated on her mood ring. It helped me to pass through the entry. Her glass "stone" mood ring was green. How could she be so calm?

The living room looked like a giant had turned the place upside down, shaken it for good measure, then righted it, leaving it utterly trashed for no reason I wanted to imagine. My mom would have a fit if our house ever got this messy. My dad would holler over all the perfectly good things being broken or left behind like this.

What happened here?

Further to the back of the trailer, I could see that the

bedding was a tangled mess. Built-in dresser drawers were opened with clothes spilling out. The bathroom was tiny, floor covered in scrunched tissues and old toothpaste containers, brushes, and bottles. The kitchen cupboards stood open, dishes flung everywhere, some broken, some littering the floor and counters. Smashed glass crunched under my wood-soled feet as I left Sue's side to look around.

The living room had upended chairs, the couch had ripped arms and a missing cushion. A macramé owl hung crookedly from a wall. Broken glass sparkled in sunlight streaming from the oversized windows, glinting off the bits of paper like diamonds. The weirdest part about the living room was the papers and photographs strewn with abandon on the goldenrod shag carpet and the tiered lamp tables. Mostly the scraps were like giant white confetti, though some photographs had been torn in half and burnt at the edges. When I bent to look closer at some of the pictures, I saw children, adults, the same people over and over with only a few new ones featured. *A family?*

I wanted to ask my sister a hundred questions to see if she understood something about the state of this place that I couldn't. We looked from the mess to each other. I saw the same puzzlement in her open mouth, squinting-in-concentration eyes that matched my own curiosity. *Who did this? Why? Why own these things and then leave them? And why are the family photos torn and burnt, discarded like bad memories?*

"Should we book it out of here?" I said, meaning to sound matter-of-fact. Instead, my voice practically squeaked.

Tea Cozies and Terabytes: People

At once Sue's bewilderment turned to disbelief at my cowardliness. Her eyes opened wide as if to declare, "Dream on!" She even laughed in the semi-mocking way my dad would when something so obvious eluded his dumb bunny children.

"How can we leave now?" she said and pulled a small notebook from her beaded purse. She loved Nancy Drew and fancied herself a detective. An excited twinkle sparked in her eyes and one of the resulting sparks hit me. Now I wanted to explore and investigate and *know*, too.

"Hot *dog*!" she said happily and rushed toward the mysterious graveyard of papers.

The next hours passed in a blur. We weren't in any hurry as we looked through the papers and wondered at the people in the pictures. Our parents were in the habit of letting us leave after breakfast and not seeing us until suppertime. We found grocery lists; letters scratched down in that mostly unreadable, grownup-man way of writing; old mail; pages ripped from books; and dated newspaper articles.

The photographs were small with a white border curled by fire or torn, black and white, grainy as if they'd been done on an Etch-a-Sketch. Each photograph was produced in a poor-quality way, washed out, damaged by the rain that probably came in through the cracked windows. In some, people in the distance were impossible to identify as they stood by what I imagined was a beach. Unknown and maybe forgotten soldiers all looked alike to me.

In my young brain, these were ancient artifacts and I an archeologist stumbling over mummies in a pyramid, or the horse and buggy of bygone days. None of it seemed real as I engrossed myself in looking at them one by one. I never thought to take note of the names on the bills. I didn't really know about bill-paying, but there were numbers with dollar signs and the papers said "electricity". My sister eagerly wrote down notes as she dug through the mess, sorting the papers into different piles.

I found a stapled, fat-stack of typed papers in a file folder. I must have watched enough courtroom or murder mysteries to know something about legal documents such as a will. I thought the line "in the event of" meant something deep and meaningful and grown-up. I liked how the words sounded in my head. I put the pages in my back pocket to keep.

Hunger gnawed at my stomach the way the enigma of the old papers gnawed at my brain. "Should we make peanut butter sandwiches and come back?" I asked, not really wanting to leave. Where was Alice with a tray of sandwiches when you needed her?

"Nah," my sister said, reaching into her purse and pulling out a red-packaged Marathon Bar.

Angelic music might well have boomed for the holy moment this turn of events inspired in me. "This is s-o-o decent," I said by way of thanks. She divided the precious candy bar in two, even giving me the big half though the treat was all hers.

Even if I was the younger one, I secretly believed I was Sue's equal. We were best friends, yet I didn't acknowledge how frequently she mothered me: singing to me when I was little so I could go back to sleep when family squabbles erupted. Making sure I didn't do anything too dumb when I engaged in things like playing with matches and melting things--a hobby of mine, rather questionable, I suppose. Or giving me the pink Huffy bike when it was intended for her, even though it meant being stuck with the red, white, and blue starred bike with the horrible banana seat. All the little things I never paid attention to because, like a mother, she did them naturally, without complaint, or need for recognition.

My now sugared senses returned full-force, and I moved around the room, turning up more interesting items: a wedding photo inside a cracked glass frame looked as if it had been painted instead of taken by a camera. The people in the picture didn't quite look real. A cloth rose was smushed under a heavy ashtray stand. Ashtrays meant matches or lighters, and I looked around for any to feed my avid melting hobby. Maybe I could try to burn some of our pictures at home so they'd look old and mysterious too.

I saw a photo album and leaned to pull it out from under the couch. As I did so, something fell out of my hands. I got on my knees and searched blindly under the furniture. For a moment, I was afraid I'd unearthed a dead mouse, but the feel of a metal chain gave me the curiosity to pull the item out. It was a white rabbit's foot on a ball chain. I wiped the dust off, alternately grossed out by the too-real feeling of bones yet captivated by the soft silkiness of the fur. Frankly, it looked more likely to bring me a curse than bring me good luck.

I decided then and there I should make a wish on it. Decisions were not my glass of Tang, and I soon had a list of fifty wishes in my head, vying to be picked #1. Big, almond-shaped eyes instead of my fat, hooded ones? A smaller nose than my pig snout? A shorter neck than my giraffe scrag? It was hard growing up and hating so many things about myself, desperately hoping I'd outgrow them all.

As I mulled the ultimate, weighty wish, my gaze shifted to my sister still nibbling her chocolate bar when mine was long gone. Jealous thoughts stole my peace. She was so many things I wasn't. Instead of trying to reach up to attain greatness, I usually ended up gathering my own unremarkable ways tighter to myself.

Squeezing the rabbit's foot, I worried I'd break the delicate bones as I prepared to present my wish to it. I recalled the legal document in my pocket and intoned in my head with great seriousness, "In the event I get out of here alive, I want to be a real grownup, free and alone and just be myself." I closed my eyes, feeling I should nod in agreement or say "amen". Nothing happened, and after waiting anxiously for a few seconds, I grew bored and looked around again for something else to do.

The ball chain would fit just right around the belt of my bell-bottoms, so I fastened it there, then opened the photo album I'd discovered earlier. Instead of seeing what was inside, my vision clouded over. A buzzing in my ears made me feel dizzy and deaf to other sounds. I smelled smoke as the first black and white photograph of the book on my lap was displayed. A child probably a few years younger than me seemed to look up at me, the boy's mouth open, eyes almost round, as if he were screaming. I half expected him to blink, he was so real- -too real- -even in colorless horror. I might as well have peeked into a room where some graphic, unspeakable act had just been carried out. I genuinely felt I had locked eyes with a living victim.

Tea Cozies and Terabytes: People

My heart rate sped up, and I was sure the sound could be heard even outside, thumping like a foot keeping the beat on a hard floor.

I turned the page to shut out the image before me. Immediately a girl appeared with the same scared look as the boy had had in the previous picture. Probably just my own wild imagination, yet I felt sure the expression both children wore in the photographs was the final moment before something terrible happened. More than anything, I wanted to show Sue what I was seeing. Aware that I was crying, I didn't want her to notice I was in tears, so I shamefully refused to look up or speak.

In a tug of war with wanting to escape the trailer and staying to solve the mystery, I found myself almost involuntarily turning the pages faster and faster because I had to know what and who else was pictured in this dreadful book. I had to see what had produced those horrified expressions, had to witness what was coming. Certain I would throw up, I nevertheless willed myself not to. *I can't hurt or soil what's left of these children,* I resolved. I had to protect them and their memory.

For once I didn't take forever to make a decision. My hands made the choice for me as I shakily removed the photographs from the book, stacked them, and put them in my other back pocket as if doing so was rescuing them from a sinking ship.

Though I'd hidden them out of sight, I could feel the heat of them against me, could smell the burnt pictures and papers I'd seen before. The smell and sensation of burning seemed to grow and make me sicker until I couldn't breathe and felt seared. On shaky, half-numb legs, I pushed myself to my feet, ready to run for fresh air.

I whirled around to tell my sister I had to leave, had to go *now!*, but she was gone. I gasped out loud. She couldn't and wouldn't have left without me, yet she was somehow gone without a trace. Paralyzed with dread, I searched the trailer despite my certainty that I would have noticed her getting up if she'd intended to leave. Oh, to call her name, call for help from anyone! My voice emerged in barely a whisper, swallowed up in fear so big I couldn't think or feel or talk around the terror seizing me from all sides.

Panic grew inside me; a hot air balloon inflated so big, it couldn't be kept from rising. The balloon threatened to float away with me until all that remained was a nameless fear and the empty sky and faces below staring up at me with wide eyes and open mouths, scared for themselves and for me. *Faces like the ones in the pictures. Yes, faces just like that, faces I just saw.*

Against my better judgment, I sank back to my knees in the shards of glass and debris. I couldn't quell my fervent curiosity. Such a thing was impossible. I had to know. I pulled the pictures from my pocket, already convinced of what I would find, urgently not wanting to see that very thing. *I don't want to. I have to.* The conflict was violent inside me.

Holding my breath, I shuffled through the sheaf of photographs. I realized I was whimpering like a little child lost. The boy, the girl, other unknown children, one by one, all wearing the same horrified look. Now I turned over a new one. My sister's eyes stared, shocked and accusing, out of the black and white photograph at me. Her mouth was open in a silent scream...

Revoked

Linda Derkez

One minute I was a ten-year-old kid living in the 70s, dressed in bell bottoms with my sister next to me snooping in an abandoned trailer. The next moment I was a 40-something in leggings with a missing sister frozen forever in a sinister photograph.

Time portal or amnesia, I had no answers for how I'd skipped over thirty years of my life to arrive back at the abandoned trailer. Maybe it was bad magic where every word we said or thought could bind us in a place worse than a prison.

My breathing came in gasps as if I'd been competing in a marathon when I'd only walked from my car across the neglected grass. It wasn't that my 40-year-old body was out of shape. More that every cell of my being reacted with terror at the sight of my nightmare's origin. As I neared the blackened husk of the bus-sized trailer, I felt sick and anxious. Yet I resolved to find my way back or to bring my sister forward in time. At the very least, I intended to find some answers. . . .

Answers to why *I* survived that day, why my then ten-year-old body had reacted to the increasing smoke by running outside for air, reviving enough to turn back and reach for the door only to find the hand in front of me foreign and adult, yet somehow my own. As a rippling had swept through me, I'd felt like I was on a carnival ride and I'd suddenly been eye level with a higher part of the door.

Just as I'd miraculously grown into an adult, the trailer had instantly grown cold and dead, as it'd been today when I found myself in Oklahoma, back on the dilapidated steps in front of the carcass of a trailer.

Perhaps my hand on the doorknob had woken me. I went from thinking I was ten to being forty. I didn't remember any memories of my life in-between. Still, I knew things. I knew my parents had died years ago. I thought I lived in my family home in Wisconsin by myself with some cats. I knew I'd driven to Oklahoma to investigate the mystery the police had never solved. I even knew this wasn't my first attempt to come back to the scene of the crime.

Looking at the remains of the trailer, I reached into my purse for my sister's old, beaded purse which was wrapped in cloth to preserve it. Inside the fake suede relic were black-and-white photographs I'd spent a lifetime studying, despite how they horrified me: pictures of missing children and adults with terrified end-of-life-as-they-know-it expressions. One of them was of my sister. She'd been beside me one second and the next she was stolen from me--from this life--and trapped and tortured inside the photograph.

Tea Cozies and Terabytes: People

I lived in a modern world now. Great technological advances had been made that seemed to have the single-minded goal of eliminating interaction with the people around us. I'd tried to copy the black and white photos, once even taking a picture of them with my fancy cell phone. Nothing seemed capable of copying the pictures. Blank paper was the result each and every time. I knew why, too. These weren't merely pieces of two-dimensional paper. They were living, breathing people in cells they'd been trapped inside. I intended to break my sister out of her prison.

Being a grownup, I'd read the contract, the will I'd found in the trailer that fateful day. The words "in the event of" had become my whole life. Not only did I realize that "in the event of" meant someone's death, I'd also googled the names in the document and found the address of the survivor.

After I visited the burnt-out trailer once again, finding no more clues then I had in any of the other countless times I'd relived this day, I drove like a programmed robot to the house of the heir of the will. I parked in the driveway of a once grand Victorian house that looked colorless against a mostly white sky. No flowers, only gray statues decorated the yard like tombstones. When I walked up to the door, I had a sickening feeling of déjà vu. Part of me believed I existed on this late spring day, this day and this day alone, as if I were caught in a loop.

Somewhere was my real life where I was a free and independent adult as I'd always dreamed. Instead of a dream come true, I lived a constant nightmare of loss and isolation because of the bizarre portal that'd become my existence.

As if I'd been expected, the door opened and a dark haired man in a blue leisure suit with a long, pointed collar greeted me. His ghostly white appearance with unhealthy darkness under his eyes put me in the mind of a funeral home director, or the prepared corpse itself. There was something unnatural about him, a smudgy fuzziness and remoteness in his manner that made him seem to be photoshopped into the scene. Even his voice was colorless, more of an echo than a real tone.

"Welcome," he said, ushering me inside. Everything about the interior of the house was old, from the scent of the suffocating air to the furniture and wallpaper. I wonder if each of my days was a recycled version of the previous instead of a new start. How many times had I discovered the same clues and thought I might be coming closer to the truth, only to have the same day replay again and again?

I couldn't be afraid--I'd done this before--and I took my place by the fire in a tall, high-backed chair next to a black rotary dial phone that reminded me of the one my parents used to own that seemed to have weighed at least ten pounds. The fact that I was sitting on my own compact cell phone that weighed mere ounces seemed impossible. I greatly desired a chance to pick up the old-fashioned receiver with its spiral cord and enjoy the reminder of being ten and talking to my grandmother or school friend like I used to.

John--for I knew his name like it'd recently been on my tongue--made small talk about the weather while my gaze kept shifting to the old phone. Finally, he left me alone to make us a pot of tea.

Tea Cozies and Terabytes: People

The shrill cry of the old-time ring of the phone should have cut through the quiet in the same way a pistol sounded firing a bullet. Instead, the frantic wail came like a welcome invitation, as if I'd come just for this purpose. I grabbed the receiver with all the eagerness I would feel snatching a child out of a fire.

"Tammy here," I said, and my voice sounded foreign to me. I still heard my ten-year-old voice in my head.

"I don't like it here," a little boy's sulky voice greeted me.

My heart went out to him. "I know," I said, "but the others are there to keep you company."

There was silence. "It's not the same," he moaned. "When is John coming?"

I leaned toward the phone's cradle. I went rigid at the boy's words. Then I said words I hadn't known were coming. "John's not coming. He's my husband now." Instantly, a cold sweat broke over me, as if the pores of my whole body were weeping. I looked down at my aging hands. Next to the old mood ring on my pinky was a diamond wedding band from a marriage ceremony I didn't recall to a man I recognized yet couldn't claim to know.

The boy's crying was unbearable, making my chest tighten to the point where I felt I might pass out. The only relief came when the line went silent. Then I heard some rummaging on the other end of the line before a voice very similar to the ten-year-old one in my head spoke. After a disorienting moment, I reminded myself I was here in the present.

"Tammy? Why didn't you become a bird to fly for help? Then I could have transformed into the wind to blow the fire away." My sister Sue was still imagining she was the boy member of *The Wonder Twins*, and we worked as a team to overcome obstacles.

I couldn't answer. I was crying and happy and grieved and frightened all at once to hear her voice.

"Why did you do it?" she asked, and I recognized somehow like an often-repeated refrain that I only recalled at the moment it was spoken. Always, she hung this question around my neck like a millstone.

John returned to the room now. He took the phone from my hand and hung the receiver up, a pleasant clattering noise I remembered fondly. He sat on the other side of the fire in the matching chair after he'd poured out the tea in his deceased mother's delicate cups.

I studied him while he looked back at me with a calmness that made me question whether I was in a play and he a familiar actor I'd seen somewhere else. Had I known him when I was a child? When he was a child? I stared and racked my brain. Then I shakily opened my purse to get out my sister's childhood purse. Methodically, I sorted through the pictures until I found the very first photo that'd haunted me at the trailer. The little boy with his mouth opened in quiet entreaty, his eyes round with fear, his likeness so real I thought he might move in the photo to turn and look right at me. This man John beside me--a colorless man in black and white, a man I called my husband--was the little boy all grown up. Though he no longer showed any fear, they were the same eyes.

"It's you," I said accusingly. I felt like I was remembering stage lines I'd practiced and practiced until I no longer needed to think to have them emerge from my mouth. "You're this boy. How did you get out?" *How will I get Sue out?*

He smiled, a controlled one, like a shrink smiles at a patient lying on his sofa that he pitied. "Yes," he said, "but, before you ask how I got free, you should ask how I came to be in the picture in the first place."

He nodded toward the phone and the instrument jarred into life as though on command. Like a robot, I reached over and brought the receiver to my ear.

"John! John!" an old woman's voice sobbed. "I'm sorry. I didn't mean it. I never really wanted to wish you away. Forgive me, John. Forgive a harried mother's reckless words. Forgive me…"

I heard a click, followed by silence so I hung up the phone. I had a vision of a tired, out-of-sorts mother holding the white rabbit's foot, the one I'd made my own regretted wish on in the trailer that long-ago day. The creepy yet softly compelling lucky charm seemed as full of death as the bones inside it. Maybe she'd been carrying it after tidying up a naughty child's mess for the hundredth time that day. Her fatigue and impatience had brought out a hasty wish: *"Oh, go away. Just leave me alone for a minute's peace and be seen and not heard."*

"Your mother?" I demanded, setting my tea down before I spilled it.

John nodded. "She tried to wish me back. When that failed, she found she could wish others away--others who could be my playmates because she feared I was lonely in that place." He sipped his tea serenely. "She even wished adults away--a soldier, a policeman--so they could rescue me."

"But they couldn't?"

John chuckled. "No. It was a bit like your cell phones today. Everyone communicating but no one talking to each other or even really *seeing* each other. Besides, they just became as trapped as I was."

"And your mother?"

"Insane." John gave another ironic laugh. "My father thought my abduction had driven her crazy, but he put up with her strange ways until the rabbit's foot went missing. She ransacked the trailer we lived in then, but never found it. My father had her taken to an asylum after that. I learned later that she eventually died there, tormented by what she did and unable to convince anyone she was telling the truth."

I leaned back in my chair to relieve the lumbar pain that being forty instead of ten gave me when I was under stress. "And your father?"

John tipped his head toward the phone and once more it rang at his command. Without hesitation, I picked up the receiver. "Hello?"

"In the event of my death," an old man stiffly read, "a family member must make a wish on a family heirloom, a rabbit's foot, to bring a friend to my lost son each year." Then the voice started over, like a recording. "In the event of my death, a family member must make a wish..."

"He knew?" I hung up. "He actually believed your mother?"

"He called me on the phone," John said, giving a little shrug as if to say, *What choice did he have?* "After my mother died, he was even more desperate to solve the mystery of my disappearance for her memory's sake."

"How?" My voice was high-pitched in my agitation. "How was he able to do that?"

John shrugged. "I think he used the rabbit's foot to wish it. I don't know. A strange magic, perhaps."

"How...?" I had to clear my voice and start over in my eagerness and sudden dread. "How did you get out? Of the picture, I mean? To get back to the present?"

John's black eyes appeared to be momentarily pupilless as his gaze burrowed into mine. His penetrating glance dug down into a remote, forgotten corner inside me. "You," he said simply, as if the answer was obvious.

"Me?" His prodding expression had the effect of a volcano in my head. All the things I'd stopped up, unable to remember properly, were flowing. My consciousness was seared by the onslaught. Guilt like fiery rivers of lava gobbling everything in its path.

As a sinner stands at the mercy of a God who'd witnessed and written down every bad deed and thought in His Book, so my sins were revealed. Without grace or forgiveness, I was driven to my knees. I reached out to feel the heat from the fireplace. *Fire!*

There'd been a fire that day. My childish hobby of setting things alight and melting them had destroyed two lives in mere moments. In the trailer, I'd found matches and used them in a ten-year-old reckless way, dropping the matches carelessly while searching through the piles of left-behind photos and papers. The smoke and flames had forced me to run for air, though all I'd wanted to do was find my mysteriously missing sister.

Filling my lungs with fresh air had stopped being my priority when flames shot out the broken windows. I'd run back for my sister, blind in my panic for her. Reaching for the door handle had transported me thirty years ahead.

How many times had I reached out to save Sue and found myself forty-years-old in a future without her?

"In the event I get out of here alive, I want to be a real grownup, free and alone where I can just be myself." My old wish had come true but not in the way I'd intended. In the same way, years before, a mother had wished her son away for one moment of peace and quiet only to regret it into a tormented senility.

I became aware of John hovering above me, and I looked up at his unfeeling face. Why had I married him? I felt no love, merely a connection. We were two lonely people with a past connection. Nothing more. The only two people who knew and believed the unbelievable thing that had happened. And yet there was more. Another reason...

John dropped the rabbit's foot in front of me. I grabbed it up like my hand was gobbling a meal. *I'll make a wish. A new wish. This time...*

I'd done this before. Over and over, I'd wished my life away to fix what I'd destroyed in a desperate bid to make things right. And I'd married John so that...

So I can be a family member! An heir to the wish and to the "lucky" heirloom.

But how had I brought him back from the other side? Not the wish alone. No, that wasn't the whole of it.

My mind tracked the answer like an animal on the scent of a hunt. *The fire!* That was it, the key.

"You thought that last time," John said in a rather superior and bored way. "That's why you destroyed your family home in Wisconsin. What you wanted to happen didn't come true. Let's dispense with your attempts to change this. In the meantime, I'll go put your car in the garage. You live here now."

Calmly, John walked away. His life in a two-dimensional world had flattened his soul. If I was able to free my sister, would she be the same way?

I'd killed my beloved sister in the accidental fire. Would she be able to return? Would she forgive me? I stood up, trembling. I had to try. Even if I had to lose my life to find hers, I had to end this existence filled with nothing but torture.

Lose a life to save another. My head jerked up in realization, and my shaking legs felt infused with the strength of steel. My sister's life had been given in exchange for John's freedom. That was the difference. That was the key I'd missed on my previous attempts to get Sue back. I understood now that a sacrifice was required to undo the strange magic that held Sue captive. I would gladly atone for my reckless, thoughtless wish by giving my life for my sister's freedom.

With a peace I hadn't known for a lifetime, I went about my final task with relief and resolve. I found kerosene and alcohol, splashing the room as if bathing it in a heady perfume. I lit a fire and knelt on the floor with the bony rabbit's foot clasped in my hand. Ceremoniously, I laid out the papers kept in my purse. The will, the black and white photos of the lost children and the others, all in order. I kept John's photo in the sequin purse since he was already back in the land of the living, though I wondered if he was really just as lost today as he was when he'd lived in the timeline inside the photograph. Holding the likeness of my sister in my other hand as the room licked at me with hungry flames I welcomed, I chanted: "In the event of my death, I freely will my life for my sister's and for these others. I wish for Sue to have a chance to be a real grownup, free and independent. I wish for her to have a full life in the real world."

As the flames ushered my life away, I turned to look beside me just as I had the day in the trailer. This time, instead of finding Sue missing, I saw her emerge in a magically flameless room, her legs stretching, her face molding with thirty years of aging. The sight should have frightened me. Instead, I welcomed her blessed presence. My pain was as insignificant as labor pains in the face of an eagerly awaited newborn. I knew I wasn't really dying because my sister was part of me and I was part of her. I would live on in her life.

As I prepared to take my last breath, I noticed the room was full of strange light that was heavenly, not due to the fire. I turned to gaze up into my sister's large eyes. I'd admired and missed those eyes for a lifetime. Her eyes reflected back to me what she saw now: A vision of me in black and white, a white frame of paper that would serve as my perpetual abode, my mouth open in wonder, expression frozen in peace and love. I'd found the way to save my sister. She was finally home.

Friends Forever

Rita Durrett

"Let me out! Come on, guys, let me out. Open this door right now, or I'll beat the living crap out of you."

I hate the dark. It makes me think of Grandpa being locked in that casket and buried under all that dirt.

Bam. Bam. Bam. My head pounded. Getting mad made it worse. I tried to calm down. The gulping of air and wheezing as it expelled finally slowed to a normal breathing.

I couldn't remember when the headaches had started. I'd been having tiny ones for at least a month, but they were getting worse. Nearly every morning I felt like throwing up. I hadn't told my parents. Mom was one of 'those' moms. If I told her I hurt or felt bad, she'd have me in the doctor's office quicker than my dog could eat his treat.

"Are you gonna unlock this door or am I gonna to have to break it?" I yelled. Perspiration trickled down my face. I wiped it on my shirt sleeve. I balled up my fists and slammed them against the door. A flash of regret zoomed through my mind. *What if it breaks? Do they send fifteen-year-olds to prison for destroying school property?* I heard snickering through the hated door and couldn't keep myself from slamming my shoulder into the unforgiving wood.

A key grated in the lock. I turned the knob, shoved, and found myself free. I rubbed my shoulder.

"We were just joking with you, Dillon. Who'd a thought you'd get so ticked off," said Conner.

My former, as of ten minutes ago, best friend Olive, glared at me as we stood toe-to-toe in the hallway. Bailey, another buddy of mine, slouched against a broom.

"If you'd been working with us instead of day dreamin' about Ashley Keys or foolin' around where you don't belong, we'd never have locked you inside the janitor's closet," said Bailey.

Both of my friends wore sweat-soaked shirts. Muddy smudges streaked their faces, and they had dirt-caked hair plastered to their heads. All three of us had been hired by Conner's dad to help him clean out our high school so the custodians could get it ready for the next year. I didn't mind workin', but findin' stuff was a lot more fun. Plus, he might have been half right about Ashley. She occupied the biggest part of my thoughts most of the time. "Yeah, well, I'd probably have locked you in, too."

I picked up a jar from the floor. "Hey, look what I found while foolin' around." It looked like a mayonnaise jar, only much bigger with thick, old-looking glass. White stuff filled up about a fourth of the container. Someone had pasted an old hand-written label reading, 'NaCN' in the middle of the bottle. "Look at this!" I pointed to the coolest thing about the label. A skull and crossbones.

Conner wrinkled his nose and squinted as he peered closer at the label. "What's NaCN?"

"I figure it's the deadliest chemical known to man," I

said. I pretended to shake some out onto Conner's head. "The teacher left it in the podium in the Chemistry room. I guess he forgot to lock it up with the rest of the chemicals."

Bailey eyed me suspiciously. He looked both ways down the hallway, like a bank robber getting ready to run. "You ain't gonna keep it, are you?" he whispered.

"Heck yeah, I'm keeping it. I'm puttin' it on my shelves with the crossbones showing."

I shook the bottle and watched the white stuff roll around inside. "It looks kinda like salt, but I'm not gonna try it."

We all agreed that would be dumb, and that even Kotter, our classmate famous for being the human garbage disposal, wouldn't taste something with a skull and crossbones on it. So I devised a plan to sneak it home. I would hide it in a box of trash and sit it out by the dumpster to pick up and take with me later in the day.

That evening, when we all piled into Conner's dad's pickup, I casually put the plan in motion. "Hey, Mr. Conner, I need an ole box for my turtle. Would it be okay for me to grab that one?" I asked, pointing to THE box.

"Sure. Jump out and get it."

So I did. My head hurt fiercely, and my breathing sounded like a basketball player after a full court press as I slid back into the seat beside Bailey, but I had the prize. I made it home, and no one but the guys knew about the crystals.

My head hurt so badly that evening I broke down and told Mom, even though I knew she'd make me go to the doctor. She did. Somehow, she managed to get an appointment the next day.

The doctor checked me all over. "Other than the headaches, has anything else out of the ordinary been going on with your body?"

"I get sick to my stomach most mornings when I get out of bed. I've been trippin' over my own feet a lot, and my eyes get all blurry when I try to read."

"Hmm."

The doctor sent me out to the waiting room while he talked to Mom. That was okay with me. I used the time to look up NaCN again on my cell phone. I'd probably read the information half a dozen times since I got home last night but couldn't resist reading it again.

"This is so cool," I said loud enough to make the other patients scowl. I read the passage again, just to refresh my brain. *"Sodium Cyanide is among the most rapidly acting of all known poisons. NaCN is a potent inhibitor of respiration. An oral dosage as small as 200–300 mg can be fatal."*

There wasn't time after that to give what I'd read much thought. Mom came out, all pale and goofy acting. She hugged and kissed me and wiped tears from her eyes as she walked with me to the car. We spent the afternoon with me being poked, prodded, and x-rayed. She wasn't talkin' much, so I had no idea what was going on. I didn't find out until later that night when she told Dad.

"I have some news. It isn't good, but we will get through this as a family."

"What are you talking about, Flora?"

"I took Dillon to the doctor today because he complained of headaches. It turns out he has a brain tumor. It's large, and it's inoperable. The doctor isn't sure what the treatment plan will be, but we're going to fight this. She paused to hug me. "Dillon, you are going to be okay."

Mother didn't sound sure about the 'okay' part. The buzzing in my ears and pulsing pain in my head prevented my hearing much else. *Brain tumor? Don't people who have inoperable brain tumors die? They are put in a box and buried six feet in the ground. Then what? Is that the end? Do they live in a blackness for all eternity?* My brain whirled, asking questions I couldn't answer.

My parents sent me to bed. I walked in a daze but found my way. My dreams fixated on being in the dark. I woke up knowing I could not go into the unknown all alone. Someone had to go with me.

The skull and crossbones jumped out at me first thing upon waking. I had a plan. Not a full, big, 'this is going to work' plan, but an inkling of a plan. It consisted of getting a plastic baggie from the kitchen and shaking enough crystals to fill a cereal spoon into the sack. My hands shook as I removed the lid. After a deep breath to steady my hands, I finished the job, zipped the bag closed, and stuffed it in my pocket.

That little bag felt like a huge softball. My brain figured everyone I passed knew I had it and knew what I was going to do. If they did, they had me beat. I had no idea, but I knew I wanted a friend to go with me when I died.

"Mrs. Breedlove?"

"Yes, Dillon?"

"May I go to the restroom?"

"Yes, but come right back. The lesson is about to start."

"Yes, Ma'am," I promised as I slipped out of the classroom door.

I wandered in the general direction of the stairway. Then I smelled it. Lunch. Stew and cinnamon rolls were on the menu. A lot of people would eat in the cafeteria today.

My hand shook a little as I grasped the handle and opened the cafeteria door wide enough to slide through. The cooks bustled around the kitchen, too busy to notice me I entered the room filled with tables and chairs. Posters admonishing healthy living lined the walls. Reading them made me angry and more determined. I noticed the ice machine on a side wall. Nearly everyone would get ice. I clumsily made my way toward the big box, my hand clutching the baggie of white crystals. The lid felt heavier than I expected, but I pushed it up.

"Mr. Dillon." The custodian's voice boomed loud and commanding from behind me.

My heart jumped and so did I. The lid slammed, making a loud echo throughout the room. "Yes, sir?" I asked as I swung around.

"What are you doing down here when you're supposed to be in class?"

"Uh, I don't know. I wanted a piece of ice."

"You shouldn't be in here. Go get a drink of water and get back to class."

"Yes, sir," I muttered as I hurried past him and out the door. The little white packet forgotten in my hurry to escape.

I walked through the English classroom door and smiled. Ashley had her feet in my chair. She moved them as I walked to my seat. She sat behind me, which turned out to be convenient. I could sit sideways and talk to her easily.

"You're late."

"I had permission," I whispered. "What are we doing?"

"Finishing where we left off reading Romeo and Juliet, starting on page 280."

I turned and read. The lesson immediately grabbed my attention. Juliet drank a potion so she would appear dead and wouldn't have to marry Paris. However, it backfired when Romeo found her and thought she was dead and poisoned himself. *I wonder if Ashley would be willing to die with me so I wouldn't have to be by myself.*

The reading no longer interested me as I thought about the packet in my pocket and sweet Ashley spending eternity by my side. *Should I ask her, or make the decision for her? Juliet didn't ask Romeo.*

Ashley solved my dilemma when she tapped me on the shoulder and quipped, "I'd never kill myself over some guy. Romeo didn't think that one through."

The question became when and how. Then I remembered the exam. "Hey, Ashley, can you come over this evening and help me study for the test over this stuff? Mom will buy us some pizza and pop."

"Yeah, I guess. About six?"

"Sounds good. I'll have it delivered at six."

A peaceful feeling settled over me. For the first time since the tumor news, I didn't feel scared.

At 5:30 my phone dinged. Ashley's picture showed up on the screen, and I answered. "Hey, what's up? I just called in the pizza. Are you on your way?"

"I'm sorry, I forgot this is my mom's birthday. We're having a family celebration. My parents won't let me come.

I've been begging for the past hour. It's still, 'no'. I'll see you tomorrow."

"Yeah, okay," I mumbled. Her loss. Not mine, but still a big disappointment.

My head hurt. I felt like throwing something. A sledgehammer pounded between my ears. Bam. Bam. Bam.

I grabbed my cell phone and tapped Connor's picture. "Hey, I've got some pizza ordered. Why don't you come on over and join me?"

"Sounds great! Can Bailey come? He's waiting here until his parents get home. My dad can drop us off on his way to the store."

"Sounds like a plan," I said.

I took the crystals from my pocket and poured them in a two liter of pop. Then I took down the skull and crossbones and added more, tossing the container in the trash.

The guys showed up just as the pizza arrived. I knew I could count on them. They were the best friends a guy could have.

"Where's your skull and crossbones bottle?" asked Bailey as he made himself comfortable on my bed.

Bam. Bam. Bam.

"I tossed it." *Did he suspect?*

Bam. Bam. Bam.

"Don't drink your pop, yet," I said. "We're going to make a toast and drink it at the same time."

"You're killing me, Smalls," quipped Conner. "I'm dying of thirst."

Bam. Bam. Bam. *Was he making a joke from the movie he liked or did he know?*

I kept my head down and blinked rapidly. Would they drink with me even if they knew? I couldn't take the chance. I needed my friends to get through this.

My. Head. Hurt. So. Bad.

I raised my head, picked up a cup, and held it out toward my friends. "Everybody grab a cup." They held their cup up to mine, smiling as I gave a toast, "To being friends forever. Drink up."

Houdini

Rita Durrett

Our dog's name is Buddy, but he should have been Houdini. A Pit Bull mix, he was generally happy playing in his water tub or standing guard on top of his dog house in his pen, located in the corner of our fairly large backyard. He much preferred the outdoors to being inside our home. A sweet and loyal companion, he wouldn't hurt anyone, but he had the strength of Hercules. He learned at an early age how to use that power. Only his true owner, my youngest son, a muscled, six-foot teen, dared take him for a walk. When that son grew up and went away to school, Buddy's exercise regimen became confined to the backyard. He handled it well, but one day something changed. I looked out the kitchen window while fixing breakfast and didn't see Buddy. I went to the door and called. No dog.

My oldest son, Brett, lived in an apartment several blocks away. I called him to go find Buddy. It wasn't long before he pulled into my driveway with the dog sitting in the front seat, his head hanging out the window, with what I'd describe as a big smile on his face. As soon as I opened the rider's side car door, Buddy jumped out, tail wagging,

Tea Cozies and Terabytes: People

and headed for the backyard. With his head at the gate of his dog pen, he rushed inside as soon as I opened it wide enough for him to fit through.

"Make sure the gate's fastened, Mom. He's a pain to get in the car."

I securely latched the gate and watched as Buddy gulped water and ate from his feeder. "Thanks, Son. It's secure. See you later." I felt relief at knowing Buddy was home and wouldn't be picked up by the pound. The city dog catcher made the rounds regularly. Animals of Buddy's breed were only kept a couple of days before being put down. Our community had deemed Pit Bulls dangerous. Buddy was not, but might behave in a manner, with strangers, and in a strange location, that would lead them to believe he was a threat.

Brett left, and I went back inside. I sat down to watch TV, only to look up and see Buddy in the backyard. I couldn't take the chance that he would stay in that enclosure any better than he was staying in his pen. I called Brett, and he came immediately. Buddy met him in front of the house.

"How'd he get out, Mom?"

"Good question, Son. I'll put him in the garage until you can find his escape hole."

Brett soon came back inside, ready to put Buddy back inside the pen. "He dug under the fence on the back side. I put a couple of cement blocks in the opening. He can't dig out, now."

I returned to my chair, and Brett went back to his apartment. Five minutes later Buddy was out again. I laughed and called my son.

"How did he dig through those blocks?" he asked. "I'm calling Richard to see if he has any ideas. I'll be over in a few minutes."

Our friend, Richard, came over and surveyed the dog pen. Together, he and my son decided the dog had picked up the blocks with his mouth and tossed them aside. They filled the hole with leftover cement from the potting shed. Both men came into the house laughing about how persistent Buddy was, confident the problem was fixed.

"He's out again," I said, looking out the kitchen window.

"What?" asked Richard, his voice incredulous.

"He can't be!" exclaimed my son. "How'd he do that?"

Brett and Richard returned to the pen, Buddy following behind. They were out in the yard at least thirty minutes before returning, once again confident the issue had been resolved.

This time my son waited before leaving for home. After a while Buddy went in his doghouse, Richard turned on a football game, and Brett left for his place. I started lunch. When I turned to the sink to wash my hands, Buddy stood on the deck, tail wagging, tongue hanging out, looking straight at me through the window. I couldn't help but chuckle.

"He's out," I said to Richard as I picked up my phone and called my son.

"You're kidding. He can't be out. How'd he do that?"

'I don't know, but I'm standing here looking at him."

"Houdini's out of the pen," I said to Brett through the phone.

Tea Cozies and Terabytes: People

"I'll be there in a minute," he muttered. A deep sigh could be heard before he hung up.

He arrived, and the two guys once again went to the dog pen. Buddy close behind, obviously enjoying all the attention his new game created.

"He dug under the front fence this time. It was the only place left. Everywhere else either had tree roots or a neighbor's wooden fence. We fixed that spot. He won't be able to get out," said Richard as he and Brett came in to eat.

"I've heard that before," I commented dryly.

Lunch over, I went to the sink to clean up and looked out the window. Sure enough, Buddy was watching me from the deck, waiting for his companions to come out and "play".

"Come on Brett. I've got an idea," commented Richard as he motioned for Brett to follow him to his pickup. When they returned, they had landscaping ties in the back. They stacked them two deep on the outside of the fence and staked them down.

"I dare that mutt to escape that," exclaimed Richard. He didn't look or sound confident.

The three of us returned to the living room to wait. I could see the front of the dog pen from my chair. Buddy checked out his escape hole but didn't seem as interested in leaving as he did earlier in the day. I think he'd tired of the game and decided to take a nap. That was the last time Houdini, I mean Buddy, managed to get out of his pen, but he certainly gave the guys fits that day.

Butterfly Mims

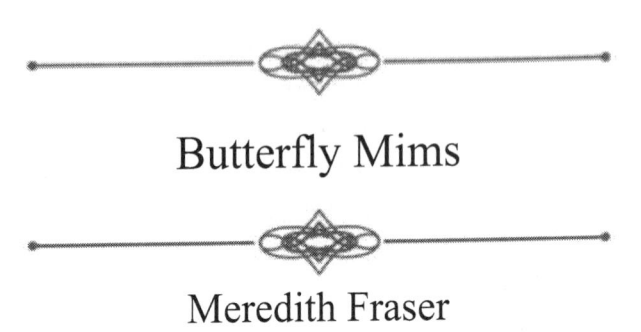

Meredith Fraser

One morning after a typical Oklahoma spring storm--you know the type: winds howling like hungry wolves, lightning cracking and thunder booming like an air raid--I awoke to a startling problem. It seems I was a prisoner in my own house. The aging Washington Hawthorne tree in our front courtyard was too weary to fight Mother Nature's elements anymore. Giving up the ghost, so to speak, its final resting place was across my front porch, courtyard, and koi fish pond.

Our neighbors are like extended family. Almost immediately, their chainsaws were eagerly chewing up the old broken guardian, allowing me to escape. Sadly, it only seemed right to acknowledge all the shade and beauty the tree had provided over the years. According to my husband though, wanting to have a proper funeral for our poor, faithful friend was a bit over the top. Instead, we just nodded a smile of thankfulness, saluted and threw some of our old friend's leaves into the wind. The next week, the tree's broken stump was claimed by an enormous machine

Tea Cozies and Terabytes: People

with gigantic teeth, eating all the wood fed to it and in return, spitting out mulch for thirsty gardens. Ashes to ashes...

Which brought me to my next dilemma. What would the next generation in the courtyard be? I decided on a cozy English garden theme complete with foxgloves, hollyhocks, and other English- sounding plants. The purpose was to inspire me to sit with a book while indulging in a wee spot of Earl Grey tea. Pinkies up. Somewhere in this wonderful scheme I momentarily forgot where I actually lived. An English garden in a treeless, southwest location made me quickly realize I had a lot to learn.

The Oklahoma sun took one look at my tender young babies and quickly fried them as if to say, "Ha! Take that!" England's climate is described as temperate maritime. Oklahoma's summer eats temperate maritime for lunch. My enormous green thumb was quickly demoted to a lime green little toe! O well, on to Plan B,

My family gave me a four- foot high statue of a little girl jumping rope. We named her Flora after the pink fairy godmother in Disney's *Sleeping Beauty* movie. My house is a "Mouse" house but that's another story. With Flora being the focal point, I decided plants that would attract butterflies and bees would be appropriate. Researching all the correct plants for attracting such delicate creatures, I chose licorice fennel, dill, milkweed, flocks, zinnias, and other plants that needed full sun. After all, fool me once.

As spring turned into summer, I was feeling pretty cocky that my green thumb had returned. The fennel I placed behind Flora erupted into an eight- foot alien plant with spiky yellow flowers and feather branches. I was sure at one point, it was eyeballing me wondering if I too, would taste like chicken. It became a quest to see just what it would become as long as it stayed away from me. The milkweed grew into massive bushes beside the alien. Flora being Flora, happily jumped rope in the midst of all the action circling her. Now we waited to see the next chapter.

The person who coined the phrase "when it rains, it pours" was spot on this time. The bees were buzzing and several varieties of swallowtail butterflies feasted on the alien's eerie blossoms. I even made a puddling station for the butterflies which consists of a shallow dish with sand, dirt, rocks, and water. The butterflies stopped on the rocks and dipped their proboscis, or tongue, into the wet sand and dirt. Their proboscis acted like a straw and sucked up water and minerals they needed. How about that? I was their own personal chef!

After all that sweet nectar and plenty of puddling, nature took its course with a fury. I began to notice caterpillars everywhere. Even the spiky alien was decorated in yellow, green, and black jewels like the Rockefeller Center Christmas Tree. I smiled as I thought, "Wonder if you taste like chicken now?"

Hundreds of caterpillars filled my garden and soon I became a neighborhood attraction. One neighbor even helped her 95-year-old mother venture over to gaze at all the hungry mouths.

And hungry those little guys were. Soon they chewed down to the nubbins on my fennel and dill. What to do? All I can say is, if you ever find a crazed looking lady buying all the parsley Walmart has, don't ask why.

Tea Cozies and Terabytes: People

Poking the parsley on any remnants of the ravaged plants was like creating a new art form. Anyone can paint or draw a tree. But to make one out of parsley and dill stumps, that takes talent! My hungry babies ate my masterpiece like one admires the Mona Lisa.

It finally dawned on me that I was truly emotionally attached to all my little charges. Like any good caregiver, I needed a name. Obviously, I wasn't their actual mother, so I decided to be their grandmother. My human grandkids call me Mims, thus Butterfly Mims was born. A name I wore like a badge of honor.

Weeks went by as they grew. Once I decided to touch one of the soft, squishy bodies only to be met with caterpillar rage. It instantly assumed an attack position, displayed its bright yellow antennae, and omitted a very unpleasant odor on my finger. I realized that they controlled the boundaries and I had just crossed one.

I began to notice there were fewer and fewer in my insect utopia. Afraid the robins were eating them, my grandmama bear instincts hit protective mode. I bought netting to place all around the courtyard. The little guys continued to disappear until I realized my babies were growing up. Cocoons were everywhere. Porch lights, the mailbox, our brick wall surrounding the courtyard and even Flora herself were all bejeweled in cocoons. Again, neighbors flocked to see all the cocoons. Daily, we inspected which ones had emptied overnight. Occasionally, we had the delight to watch them emerge from their slumbering beds and begin a new chapter by drying off those beautiful wings.

Monarchs, swallowtails, and various other beauties emerged and floated toward the sky like fairies dancing towards the heavens. Sadly, I went out one last time thinking okay, just like human parenting, you raise them to go out in the world and be wonderful individuals. Alas, this sentiment didn't help much more than it did with my own kids. Suddenly, one sparkling orange monarch emerged from the aftermath left behind. It gently floated towards me then started fluttering around, almost circling me. As it floated off on those gossamer wings, I swear I heard it say, "Thanks, Mims! See ya next year."

Rock Chalk Jayhawk KU

Pepper Hume

The University of Kansas. Ah yes, good ole flat Kansas, as though the mountains of Colorado pile up right against the Kansas border to drop suddenly to the Kansas plains. Same phenomenon happens on the other side with the Missouri Ozarks and the hills around Kansas City, often called the San Francisco of the Midwest. Granted, two-thirds of Kansas does resemble a slightly tilted billiard table. However, that plain also stretches halfway across Colorado, almost to Denver, from whence, looking east, you can see the curvature of the earth. Don't ever drop a billiard ball in Denver; it would roll to Topeka! East of Topeka, Lawrence lies in another world entirely, a world of green hills. And the University of Kansas.

When you go onto the campus of KU, you say you are going "on the hill." Which can, every winter, involve slogging through at least a foot of snow. Uphill! Both ways! Entirely likely on a campus which has long since spread beyond the single street along the ridge and down both sides of the steep U-shaped hill it originally crested. (Ice storms are really murder!) No wonder KU has always excelled at track sports. Even coeds develop calves of steel. Mine took years to return to normal.

What freshman with a camera could resist those buttons in the Student Union elevator?

3
2
1
B
SB
SSB

Outside the back door of the sub-sub-basement it's still a rather steep slope down to the street behind the building.

Similarly, the front door of my seven-storey freshman dorm was on the fourth floor. From the basement-level back door the next street was at least another fifteen feet lower. This gave the street alongside the narrow end of the building a five-storey climb in one block! Guess which street had the stop sign at the top of that block.

But I digress.

Doctor Goff

The pictures in my mind of Doctor Lewin Goff may not sound complimentary, although they really are. Doctor Goff was Director of the University Theatre Department from 1955 to 1967; I was a student there from 1957 to 1961. Normal protocol of the time required proper address, so he was always Doctor Goff to students, but there was no trace of distant formality about the man. For all his national renown and acknowledged genius as a theatre practitioner and educator, he hardly suited the image one would expect to go with such a reputation.

I remember a small, tightly wound dynamo, incapable of real stillness. He almost gave off that sixty-cycle hum you feel more than hear around electrical transformers. Not to say he jittered about meaninglessly. You just sensed vibrations emanating from an intensely focused mind stuck in high gear. Whether teaching, directing or merely chatting, he LOOKED at you with startling dark eyes. He gave you his full attention and cared what you thought, what you did. He had a splendid face--clean sharp-edged planes, nose and jaw of great power, wide mobile mouth, and those electric eyes. Sable hair, as irrepressible as he was topped off the whole package. Like a bird darting from one vantage point to another, he probably came as close as any human being could to seeing all sides of you and what you were doing.

My first memory of him, he was directing a rehearsal of something or other in a large converted classroom where several slender poles interrupted the playing space. He had shinnied up one of those miserable poles to get a different perspective of what his actors were doing. I can still see him, legs wrapped around the pole, leaning out sideways, nearly dislocating his jaw as he stretched farther to get a better view, his whole being focused on the action. He looked exactly like an intelligent Rhesus monkey, all snappy dark eyes and fierce attention.

During my tenure as a student at KU, the already legendary British director Tyrone Guthrie was planning to build a splendid theatre in the hinterlands of the US. He had recently founded the Stratford Festival of Canada, which remains a formidable bastion of great theatre. Declaring himself to be "anti-Broadway and anti-West End" (the British equivalent of Broadway) he was determined to spread fine theatre beyond those confines. He narrowed down the list of U.S. cities vying to become home of the Guthrie Theatre and made a grand tour to visit every one of the twenty-five finalists. His visit to Kansas City included a little side trip to nearby KU, a bigger thrill for theatre students than a visit from the Queen or the President.

Guthrie stood six-foot-four, could have passed for Charles de Gaulle, and moved with the self-conscious dignity of an ocean liner. What fun it was to watch our dear little organ grinder monkey leading the majestic *Ile de France* around the building. I did eventually forgive Doctor Goff for introducing me to Guthrie when I was wearing my most disgusting shop grubbies and a significant amount of paint, sawdust, and dirt. The big man smiled at me most politely.

As a design major and only occasionally a bit player on stage, I had much less direct contact with Doctor Goff than did the acting and directing majors. My Theatre Design major, a joint venture with the Art Department of the separate Fine Arts School, limited me to introductory theatre courses as a freshman, followed by design and art studies, none of which he taught. Nonetheless, Doctor Goff always knew who I was and kept track of what I was doing. I learned from him the compulsion to look at something from all sides. At once if at all possible. I have always stood in awe of his curiosity - intellectual, artistic, insatiable.

Tea Cozies and Terabytes: People

My First Nude Model

I'm not sure I ever knew his name. We were brand-new freshmen in our first college art class, eight o'clock, Monday morning—Life Drawing 101. The minute he came in wearing a tired old bathrobe, my friend Judy covered her eyes and whispered, "Tell me when he's naked." I never let her live that one down.

I'd like to report I behaved in a coolly dispassionate and professional manner. I certainly wanted to. I was not about to admit I was as nervous as Judy. *Don't think about him being naked*, I told myself. *This is just another subject to draw, a model for the art I am going to put on the pages of my nice, big newsprint pad. No different from models I've drawn before. Except, this time there won't even be a leotard to obscure the bone and muscle structure we'll be studying. (Why did they always have to wear black ones which hid all structural detail?) Won't be a person, just a subject. Be cool.*

I dared glance at him as he waited for everyone to settle down. He was older than any of us, Negro, but not very dark, of average height and build, all in all, perfectly ordinary. Ordinary and ugly. A man so ugly, you'd notice if you saw him on the street. Both his hairline and skull sloped back above droopy-lidded, muddy eyes. Huge lips overhung a receding chin. The nose in between was wide, but otherwise unremarkable. His close-cropped hair looked like bits of lint stuck on his skull.

My virginal, white, Midwestern stomach fluttered anyway as the instructor introduced him and directed him where to stand. Part of being cool involved not riveting my eyes on the soon-to-be naked man. Between readjusting the angle of my newsprint pad and the instructor moving around coaching his pose, I didn't actually see him until he was posed, all naked and still. Well, not fully naked; he wore a pouch.

I hope my mouth did not hang open as I marveled. None of the male nudes pictured in my new art history book displayed any finer proportions, muscular definition, or even skin texture. Not the Greeks nor the Romans nor the Renaissance. But really! How could God have put such an ugly head on such a beautiful body?

I'm sure many of my white freshman classmates were as discomfited as Judy at being allowed—no, required—to stare long and hard at a man, a Negro at that, with no clothes on. This *was* the 1950s. I suspect being the subject of such discomfort was nothing new to him. But I do wonder if I was the only one whose reaction contained that additional shock. I reminded myself this was *figure* drawing class, after all, not portraiture. Appreciate the fact that the subject we had been given was classically beautiful.

We got used to the presence of someone who was nude being among us while we were all dressed, and got on with the business of really learning to draw. In the course of our three-mornings-a-week class, we got to work on several models of both sexes and various ages. None of the others took any interest in our work during their breaks. They either remained aloof or got too friendly and chatty during a pose which distracted everyone else. One woman was so prone to conversation, she would forget herself and start to gesture as she talked.

All in all, I think our first model remained everyone's favorite, even Judy's. Not only did he have the best male body, he was steadiest at holding a pose without "falling out of it" as well as returning to it accurately after a break. All business when on the posing stand, during breaks he would stroll around with his bathrobe on, and look at the drawings. His remarks were observant but gentle, encouraging without being fatuous.

"You seem to be havin' trouble with that spot there," he said quietly to the boy next to me. He twisted his head to allow the boy to study a neck tendon up close. He suggested the boy feel the tension where the tendon met his collarbone. After the boy reworked his drawing a bit, both of them smiled at the problem solved. He was too discreet to ever invite a girl to touch him.

I took several semesters of life drawing, but never saw my favorite model again after our first semester. Can't help but wonder if the faculty reserved him for only freshmen, to break them into dealing with the nude so smoothly.

My First Lost Love

I kept having to remind myself. He was gay. He was gorgeous. He was gay. He was great fun. He was gay. He was a swell dancer. He was gay. He was a pretty good kisser. He was gay. He was the one that got away.

Or so I thought. I didn't understand then that he was never available to me in the first place. Nor did I realize it was not something he had any control over. He liked me, he enjoyed my company, we made a cute and lively couple on the dance floor or at a party, had a lot of fun. He just never took me seriously.

Hindsight being good ole 20/20, I now understand why nobody did. I never allowed them to. Like Jimmy's sexual orientation I believed my frivolous persona was inevitable. Look at what I had to work with: I was small, thin, pale, blonde, big blue eyes, soprano. My intelligence, vigorous health, and endurance were invisible. Even in high school theatrics, I learned I'd never be taken seriously for the meatier, more interesting roles. I even looked several years younger than I was. Always have. I could see my future onstage consisted of playing silly little ingénues until forever. Boring. No thanks. I channeled my penchant for drawing and painting into scenery design. Being a fey little wisp didn't matter there.

It didn't matter with Jimmy either. It fit right into his cover, as he played the silly lightweight, too. The Scarlet Pimpernel had nothing on either of us. We could've taken our show on the road.

Without thinking about it at the time, I knew behind the facade he was as serious about his music as I was about my art. I must have spent hours jammed in a practice room with him and his marimba. Luckily the size of such an instrument required one of the larger rooms. (Most were truly claustrophobic.) Lying on the floor under a marimba being played is a rare and delicious experience, especially in such a closed space! Watching him play was even better, how he manipulated two mallets with each hand, varying the distance and angle between them, hitting the right bars without looking, switching to different mallets... Sadly, even the largest practice room in the building allowed no room to deploy a drawing pad. Nor were outsiders allowed in orchestra rehearsals, so I never managed to draw Jimmy at work.

Girls who hung around with gays were likely to be called fag hags at the time. Perhaps straight guys who might have been interested in dating me were put off by my association with Jimmy. I didn't care. He had so many qualities which suited me. I thought our unspoken bond of dedication to our art and having fun would be enough. Neither of us was interested in politics or that whole collegiate fraternity/sorority scene. I fancied us Bohemians, albeit a middle class, middle American, rather clean-cut, Walt Disney sort of Bohemians.

Jimmy tired of the masquerade before I did. He began spending more and more of his free time with some guy rather than me. There were several awkward little scenes, the details of which I have managed to forget. I don't even think there was ever a big final blowout. I simply stopped being invited to marimba practice or dances.

Not to worry, I survived. Between my art and theatre classes, there were plenty of guys whose interests coincided with mine. Remember the boy next to me in my freshman life drawing class? After graduation, I married him.

A Red Tri Aussie

Pepper Hume

"But Toby is lonesome. Look how much happier you and I are together than we ever were alone."

"He's a dog!"

"Dogs are social creatures, just like us humans." Rob put his arms around me and nuzzled his beard in my hair. Luckily we were both in for the night so I wouldn't have to salvage the nice smooth bob I had recently achieved. He continued talking into the mess he also continued to make of my hair, "You go out regularly with your gal pals like I do with my writing group."

"Yet we always have each other to come home to. I get your drift there, which for a writer, is rather crude. You need to work on that. Now, let me get out of these boots and all."

He released me and plopped onto the bed to watch me change clothes. I'll never know how Toby can always tell when Rob hits that bed. True to form, a flurry of long, black, silky hair, accented with patches of caramel and brilliant white, burst in and lunged onto the bed to snuggle with Rob. All four white paws gracefully flailed about and the black-nosed, white muzzle flashed every which way as he tried to catch Rob's hands, and yet avoid them in a game only the two of them understood. Watching how possessively the dog patted and played with his human, I could well imagine he might consider me a rival for the affections of that human.

Dangerous ground there, Cyn, I told myself. That's an argument for their side. Time to counterattack instead.

"And how is that different from your taking Toby to the dog park to play with all his friends? I've been there too, ya know. He must have a dozen pals there."

"Apart from the obvious difference in cognitive understanding, I do well to get him to the dog park once a week and you can't count on those others to be there at the same time. Sometimes none of them are there at all. You haven't seen his disappointment, Cyn, nor how he mopes around when we come home."

I could see we were going to have this... discussion in various forms until I gave in. One good-sized dog in the house ought to be enough for a cat person to deal with, especially when married to someone allergic to cats. Granted, most of the dog-related duties were handled by the dog person in the house, but would two dogs satisfy that dog person? Would there be another campaign down the road for a third? I slipped my favorite house gown over my head to hide what was probably showing on my face. Too late, he'd seen it.

"It wouldn't hurt you to look," he said low and soft. I was a dead duck.

He already had the photos from Craigslist showing on his monitor. The handsome face of a red tricolor Aussie filled the screen. Naturally, the cheek patches of caramel tan didn't stand out as sharply against its red coat as they did to Toby's black. It did sport a white blaze between the eyes and down to the white muzzle nearly identical to Toby's. The animal's eyes were not the deep, rich brown of Toby's, but almost the same rusty red as its coat. Rob let me stare into those eyes a while before clicking to a full-length side shot that showed it to be every bit a classic, tricolor Australian shepherd. Where Toby was glossy black, this dog glowed with the deep red of an Irish setter. Its white ruff was not as broad as his, nor did the white of its feet stretch quite as high up the front legs. Nonetheless, even I could see how the two of them prancing along on tandem leashes would stop traffic.

Can you be a double dead duck?

The people who had put the dog on Craigslist met us out at the quieter edge of a large supermarket parking lot. We had left Toby at home. He expected any trip in the car to take him to the dog park so his enthusiasm might overwhelm a stranger. That turned out to be a good call.

After the usual greeting and chitchat, the man opened the side door of his van and started talking to the animal inside. The woman stayed near us and I soon realized why.

"Like Donny told you on the phone, we don't know nothin' about this dog, where he come from, nothin'. He just turned up in our barn. It had been raining a few days before so we figured he'd been in there since then. Skin and bone and so spooked he wouldn't let nobody come near him. We put food down and water, but he wouldn't go near it if we were anywhere around. Once he started eatin' good, he filled out a little and you could see he was a real purty dog. We showed our vet some pictures of him. He told us what breed he was, probably purebred, and somebody might pay a reward for finding him. We advertised in the paper and the Blue Sheet, but nobody ever claimed him."

Her husband climbed back out of the van, holding a leash that led back inside. He seemed a little sheepish saying, "Riding in the van, with strange noises and all, he's gotten a little scared. He'll calm down in a bit." He sat down on the door sill and leaned back inside to coax the animal.

His wife moved nervously, this wasn't going as smoothly as she had hoped. Rob noticed.

"In your listing you said you couldn't keep the dog since you raise chickens or something?"

She nodded and hugged her arms around herself. It was getting a little late in the afternoon and the wind had picked up a chill. I wasn't too keen myself on letting this drag out too long. Even though I'm not a dog person, I do know that talking to one isn't all that different than talking to a cat. I strolled over quietly to sit beside the man in the side door of his van. I didn't even look inside. I started talking, just nattering really, so the dog would get used to my presence and my voice.

"I know what you mean. When we went to meet Toby, he wasn't at all sure he wanted anything to do with us. The man had even suggested muzzling him before bringing him in from the garage. He had a heavy collar on him and he kept the leash short and tight. I knew right then that was the wrong house for that dog!"

Rob caught on to my plan and came to stand near enough for the dog inside to hear his voice as well. "We sat down at their breakfast table so as to be less threatening. Toby was pretty scared that day, too. Cyn's something of a dog whisperer and she started talking to him, all soft and quiet. Didn't take her long to get him to sniff her hand. Pretty soon she was stroking his head. She knows just where they like it. The guy was so fascinated he let her take the leash from him and was amazed when Toby sat down at her feet. I figured she'd won the day."

"And then you almost blew it by standing up too quickly," I added.

"Fast as lightning, he'd nipped me on the leg. You notice, today I was smart enough not to wear shorts."

I stifled a laugh, didn't want to startle the dog inside the van. "Those two people both inhaled so sharply, I'm surprised there was any oxygen left in the room. They must have thought the whole deal had gone south and we might sue as well."

"I just rubbed the spot and chuckled, and sat back down," Rob said. "He hadn't even broken the skin. Brought it on myself,' I said. 'But best we get this fellow home and settled in before bedtime.'"

I picked up the story. "We couldn't get him out of that house fast enough! Bundling him into our car took all three of us, but the guy was so glad to get rid of him before anything else happened, he was very helpful."

Donny had been watching the dog inside. He reached in and managed to ruffle its ears, although I could see the dog gave no response. At least he didn't recoil. "See, Rusty? They're nice people. They won't hurt you. I think we might get him out of here, now."

Rob and I stood back as Donny managed to get Rusty out of the van. The dog crouched down to the ground close beside him, and peered slantwise at us. He may have trusted that man but nothing else in this world. To see such a fine animal so beaten down, so fearful, broke my heart. In that moment, I knew that while Toby was solely Rob's dog, Rusty was going to be mine. If only for this one precious baby, I had just become a dog person.

Wondrously gentle and slow, Danny led Rusty to our car. His wife joined the trek so the dog would feel sheltered on both sides. Even so, Rusty dragged his belly on the ground every inch of the way. They had to lift him into the back seat. He didn't exactly resist, but he certainly didn't help. Much as I wanted to cradle the poor baby in my arms, I knew it would not console him. Not yet.

They gave us all the papers from the vet, hugged us and thanked us for giving him a good home and we said goodbye. We were now a two-Aussie household.

Rob carried Rusty into the backyard and sat down with him to meet Toby. As expected, Rusty shivered against Rob until Toby had completed his inspection and decided he was okay. Twice, Toby assumed the "let's play" posture—both front legs flat on the ground to the elbow, fanny high in the air. If Rusty recognized the invitation, he wasn't ready to leave his new shelter in Rob's lap just yet. Toby wandered off to check something or other. Rusty settled into Rob's lap which produced a big grin on Rob's face. Enjoy it while you can, big boy, I thought. That dog is mine.

The third time Toby came close enough to commune and then run off somewhere, Rusty very carefully rose out of Rob's lap and followed, slowly but clearly curious as to what Toby was about. Toby continued to invite and encourage. Rusty continued to hesitate and reserve judgment. Rob gave up watching and came in to fix their dinner.

I wish I could put what my writer husband calls a button on Rusty's life story with "happily ever after" at this point, but that seemed to elude us. Much as we both vied for Rusty's affection—I didn't think Rob had realized I intended for Rusty to be my dog—he still gave us the Greta Garbo "I just vant to be alone" attitude. Yes, he did learn to play a little with Toby. Yes, he enjoyed our big backyard and the comfort of being inside at night and when it rained. But no, he never seemed to enjoy being petted or snuggled. And no, he never seemed to feel at home. More than once I watched him trace the perimeter of the back yard fence as though checking for an escape hole. He endured my daily brushing, but seldom looked at me no matter how much I talked to him and petted him. He seldom came to me when I spoke to him and never came voluntarily. Even though going out the front door on leash to the car meant going to the dog park, he still strained to make a dash for freedom every time.

Came the day he managed to yank the leash out of my hand and make that dash, right across the road, busy with evening homebound traffic, and up the drive toward the Richards' house set far back behind an absurdly deep and wide field of grass. I had to wait for several cars to pass before I could cross after him. By then, he had disappeared into the woods that wrapped around both sides and behind their house. As soon as Rob had stowed Toby, he joined me in the search, both of us calling the dog's name, knowing how pointless that was.

Deep in the woods I finally spotted Rusty. He turned to look at me and I started talking to him, hoping to keep his attention long enough to reach the trailing end of his leash.

He had no intention of allowing that to happen and turned to keep out of my reach. His plan was thwarted however by the loop end of the leash being snagged on a stub of root.

"So that's why you let me get this close, you scallywag. You had no choice." I had one chance to capture that loop before he managed to tug it loose. Despite knowing it would spook him all the more, I rushed to where the leash was caught and stomped a foot on it just beyond the loop. That gave me time to release the loop from the root stub and get my hand stuck through it securely. Rusty pulled with all his might, but I managed to hold my ground. He didn't like it one bit, but he allowed me to lead him back to the car. We were still going to that dog park.

He romped around with the other dogs as usual, but I noticed he also tracked around the fence as he did at home, watching the woods beyond. Catching him to leash up to go home was no more troublesome than any other time. After dinner, Rob gave Toby his daily brushing and turned to Rusty, who endured being brushed with the same defeated attitude with which he accepted all our attention. As always, Rob talked to him the entire time he was brushing him, but tonight his voice was sad.

"When are you going to accept us as your friends, pretty boy? Nobody here will ever hurt you. Don't you like the food? Don't you like having a great big yard to play in and Toby to hang out with? Doesn't this feel good? Toby especially likes it under the chin, right there. Why don't you? I know you had a rough time of it there for a while, but you have a home now, a family. You're safe here, you don't need to run away any more. Let us love you."

When Rob finished brushing and released Rusty, the

dog went out his door without so much as a thank you. Rob stayed on the floor and watched him go. Toby had joined me on the couch but went back to Rob since he still had the brush in his hand.

"What really disappoints me," Rob said as he absently brushed the already shining black pelt. "is how cool he still is with Toby. How long is it going to take to win his trust?" He looked up at me with a thoughtful frown and stretched out on the floor. Toby snuggled against him. "When I saw all the effort you are making to get him to bond with you, I figured we had a perfect little family set up going here. I don't know what else to do."

"Like the song says, the only way 'to handle a woman is to love her. Simply love her, love her, love her.' It's true with cats. Must be true with dogs, too. Maybe some dogs just take longer. He'll come around eventually. Dogs are easier to win over than cats." I added that last more in hope than conviction.

Weeks went by as weeks are wont to do, while we made baby steps of progress with Rusty. Either he had given up trying to jump ship on the way to and from the dog park or we were more vigilant in leash control. He accepted being brushed with somewhat better grace. He ate well and continued to grow into the magnificent beast he was born to be. Yet he still lacked the pride and grace that Toby had in spades. He still went through each day without enthusiasm. I know what "hang dog" means.

"Do you realize we have never heard Rusty bark?" Rob made this observation after Toby had loudly proclaimed the presence of some small animal outside the fence in the dark.

"Count your blessings," was my reply. "I'm just glad

we have no neighbors nearer than the Richards across the road. YOUR dog would be the scourge of any normal neighborhood."

More weeks went by and we settled into what seemed to be a normal routine with one very enthusiastic dog and one very disinterested one. Until the day we came home from work to find only one dog in the back yard. We searched the entire house and all the yard. I closely surveyed the fence line and gates, paying particular attention to where the fence met the garage and the corners of the house. Then I spotted the gap under the house behind a bush. This house was old, dating from the days when they built them up on pilings of almost a foot and a half off the ground rather than flat on concrete slabs. We'd blocked up this gap across the back of the house with assorted plywood and what not when we first moved in to keep critters out of the yard. A determined dog could crawl under this house. Apparently a really determined dog had managed to move aside a piece of lattice and do just that.

With little hope we broadened our search. We consulted the Richards, the church office beyond the stand of woods on the one side of our house and hopelessly scanned the pasture that stretched over a dozen acres on the other side. For several days we fearfully watched the road, but no carcass larger than a raccoon appeared for miles in either direction.

Then one evening, Mrs. Richards called to say she'd seen a red dog on the dirt road along the side of their property that led to a clearing way in the back. I was welcome to come and watch for him to pass that way again. I took a lawn chair, a book, and a leash. Luckily, the weather held comfortably warm and dry. The fifth evening of my vigil he trotted down the road only a few yards away. I called out "Rusty" and stood up. He stopped, looked at me, and calmly continued on his way.

Two evenings later, I saw him again. I could hardly believe it was the same beaten-down dog we'd worked so hard to reassure, to make him feel safe. This fellow trotted along with his head held high, proud and confident. He was almost gone before I thought to call him. Again he stopped to look at me. He barked once and went on as before. It was the only time I had ever heard him bark. It was also the last time he took that route.

We never saw Rusty again and had to give up any hope of reclaiming him. We could not guess what he found to eat or how long he lived. Those woods were full of wild animals, some dangerous, some just nasty-tempered. Didn't matter. However long he lived, it was the life he chose. He had found his own happiness living wild and free.

Grace

Glen Mason

"As we surround this table, Lord . . ." I heard my grandma say,
In the kitchen of her rural home, whenever she would pray
Before the meals that she prepared with wood stove fires burning.
Amidst the bounty, blessings, gifts, our humble thanks returning.

Grandpa was a reverend, preacher; farmer, in constant motion.
He taught the Bible, preached the gospel, led daily devotion.
But when it came to saying grace, he knew that she was able
To praise the Lord and offer thanks, "As we surround the table . . ."

The biggest meals to loved ones served, no single effort spared.
The longest table, set on both sides, for family prepared.
Aunts, uncles, cousins, babies new, parents; all families stable.
Our Grandma reigned with loving cheer, "As we surround this table . . ."

Half century gone since the last meal prepared upon that farm.
The buildings fell, the wood decayed, old age has done its harm.
I'll not forget, her every grace began this self-same way.
"As we surround this table, Lord . . ." Her love shines on us today.

Old Doctor Palmer

Glen Mason

Old Doctor Palmer, the bringer of healing with strong, sure, and comforting hands;
He carried the black bag, the symbol of learning whose straps seem as strong as steel bands.
With calm self-assurance, he treats even the youngest who ail with unknown diseases.
Now you're treated for earache, for sore throat and coughing, for fever and incessant sneezes.
Take all his advice, "Don't ever forget that all pain is only a warning.
Even if you feel better, keep unbroken bed rest, then get up and call in the morning."

>Most commonly flu, penicillin will do
>The kindly old man gives an aspirin or two,
>He will advise you some hot tea to brew.

The community knows him, he travels the back roads in his pale yellow luxury car.

The '52 Chrysler announces his coming, we know him from down the road far.
House calls are two dollars, if you can afford it, or just work a deal out in trade.
Diagnoses and treatments were just like the kind that were previously made
In earlier dark days when TB was consumption, and "hard arteries" altered your mood,
He could just hold your hand, the only known treatment for the dark ills that always ensued.

    His records and papers say you just had the vapors.
    No such thing as Alzheimer's, you're just an old-timer.
    If blood pressure's high, just relax, you must try.

I remember the morning, then a six-year-old child, I went on a Saturday's gloom;
There Old Doctor Palmer turned his office on Main Street into a make-shift surgery room.
My mother, she brought me to this office on Main Street for reasons she dared not reveal.
The smell of the ether must surely be poison, the sound of the blood pump's low squeal.
For sixty-four dollars, cost of the procedure, we went into debt for a year.
The long convalescence, the routine health setbacks, a miracle that I'm still here.

Tea Cozies and Terabytes: People

Longstanding tradition to treat a condition;
Of chronic low fever, the only reliever
This mild operation brings pain's long duration.

Love Me No Less

Glen Mason

Love me no less that I'm crying. Love me no less when I fall.
I'm learning so fast in my childhood, but at times I forget almost all.
I take up your every minute; you can't let me out of your sight.
I'll get everything into trouble. I'll never do anything right.

Love me no less that I struggle. Love me no less when I fail.
When lessons come harder than they should, and report cards arrive in the mail.
Can I tell you I'll try even harder? Would you believe the tests make no sense?
Love me no less when I tell you my life is becoming too tense.

Tea Cozies and Terabytes: People

Love me no less in my trials. Love me no less when it's hard
To live in the world that's so hostile, when I'm constantly thrown off my guard.
They don't tell you anything helpful. They ask for too much for their wares.
I live on the edge of survival, and constantly hide from their stares.

Love me no less when I'm aging. Love me no less when I'm gray.
You loved me when we were both youthful; when old age seemed so far away.
I can't care for you like I used to. I can't show you hilltops and thrills.
Love me no less when life's color fades. We must face reality's ills.

Love me no more when departed. Love me no more than before.
Don't say I'm a much greater person, now that I can't fail anymore.
You could have reached out in those times when I could still hear the blessings you give.
Love me no more, now in heaven. Love me no less while I live.

The Trash Truck Comes at Nine

Glen Mason

New neighbor moved in just next door.
I'll try to be friendly, helpful.
    Exchange first names, maybe chat a while,
And show him the lay of the land.
    "That neighbor's real quiet." "She works at a bank."
    "That house is still empty, probably asking too much."
"Taxes aren't too high. Your new landlord's a jerk;
And the trash truck comes at nine.
    Did you get power turned on? Is the water still running?
    On days when you're lucky, the mail will be here by
three,
And the trash truck comes at nine."
    The trash truck comes at nine.

It disappoints me when I'm writing.
I mean I disappoint myself.
    It doesn't sound, down on paper, like it did in my head.
Improvements don't come when they're needed.
    My most favorite phrases won't fit in the story.
    Should I force words to fit 'til they scream?

Tea Cozies and Terabytes: People

No, my soul must sacrifice its most favorite passages,
And the trash truck comes at nine.
   The paper's been piling like an indoor landfill.
   Keep one-tenth, the rest has a place
'Cause the trash truck comes at nine.
   Yes, the trash truck comes at nine.

Have you heard, "the child is the father of the man"?
It's true, and I'm here to say, he is one cruel master.
   Sorrows, regrets, slights, and memories of insults ring.
But to seek vengeance or even think it
   Hurts the chest, the head, weakens muscles, dulls thoughts.
   Can't expect apologies, atonement, ashes or sackcloth.
That oozing, dripping sack of pain? Got to go somewhere,
And the trash truck comes at nine.
   Is it really so simple? To free your own soul,
   From heaviness and worry? We'll see.
'Cause the trash truck comes at nine.
   The trash truck comes at nine.

Space Cowboy

Jayleen Mayes

It's a warm Friday night and my kids are staying with their grandparents. It sounds like the start of a great weekend for any single parent; freedom to do as I please, eat or drink whatever I choose, sleep in. But single parents don't *really* get a night off. That's the stuff of fairytales or romance novels.

Instead of a night on the town, I'm driving a group of senior citizens to a concert in a small passenger bus which I refer to as "Ol' Bessie". They all live at the retirement community where I work, and this particular bunch have waited for this concert - part of our small city's annual OK Mozart Festival - all year. They chatter away about the guest artists, ask questions about the new shopping center, wonder where my kids are hiding for the night, and inquire if I'll be attending the concert with them.

"Oh no, I've got some work to catch up on," I tell them as I pull into the venue.

This is not completely true. I do have some work, but I'm more interested in having time to myself. My thoughts are carried away with ideas about shopping, having drinks with friends, or a quiet dinner with my book. This makes me giggle because I'm more likely to go home and change into my pajamas, watch TV for two hours, then return to take them back home. I really do lead a glamorous life.

It takes about five minutes to get everyone and their assistive devices unloaded. As I pull away, the thought of going home to Ramen Noodles, dirty laundry, and my TV actually depresses me. I pull back to the curb, do a quick calculation on my phone to check my financial situation, and decide I can treat myself to dinner out. It can't be anything too expensive, but not having to cook and being able to "people watch" sounds appealing.

The concert is downtown and the weather is pleasant so I find a safe place a couple blocks away to park Ol' Bessie and hit the streets to find a restaurant.

The downtown sidewalks are bustling with people. We have guest artists from all over the country here to perform, and many of them bring their families. Almost every room of every hotel is booked by people who have traveled to attend this annual event. Local shops and vendors are taking advantage of the extra traffic and keep their stores open later than usual. I wade my way through the crowds, almost knocking over a small toddler that escapes the grip of her not-so-attentive father. Finally I settle on a family-owned restaurant called The Painted Pony.

The place is busy, and since I'm alone the hostess suggests I eat at the bar rather than wait for a table. I agree, though secretly I know I'm being pushed off to the "can't find a date" section of the restaurant. When I order just water, the bartender is less than thrilled but perks up when she finds out I'll be eating as well. After placing my order I pull out my Kindle and become invisible. No one notices the single girl at the bar, sipping water and staring at a Kindle, so I am free to read, people watch, and maybe even eavesdrop.

Shortly after my sweet, bourbon glazed chicken arrives, a couple in their late 60s sits at the bar a few seats down from me. The owner of the establishment, Mike, is behind the bar and greets them like old friends. They order Moscow Mules and hamburgers, then engage in jovial conversation while I put my nose back to my book. I mindlessly fork food into my mouth as I try to concentrate on what I'm reading. There is some commotion at the front door as several people leave and a man in his late 30s or early 40s makes his way through the crowd toward the bar. He is average height with blue eyes and short blonde hair. I notice a ring-shaped impression around his head, probably from wearing some type of hat. As he is sitting down with the older couple, he sees me watching him and he flashes a smile. I smile as well but quickly turn back to my Kindle as the heat begins to rise in my cheeks. There is an empty chair between us, but I can smell the musky suede and Old Spice wafting off of him. It reminds me of backroads, rodeos, and dancing at Cavalcade, a western bar in Tulsa. He orders a tap beer that the owner recommends, and a chicken salad sandwich with sweet potato fries.

After a few bites he tells the owner, "This croissant is chewy."

"Hmmm. Can I touch it?" Mike asks.

As he pushes his plate across the bar, I notice he isn't wearing a ring. Yes, I may prefer to be invisible today, but I'm still single, so of course I look!

Tea Cozies and Terabytes: People

Mike pokes at the sandwich a couple times and says, "No, that's not right," and whisks the plate away to the kitchen.

The guy notices me watching this exchange. I am aware of how blushed my cheeks are probably getting.

"Seems like what you pay for chicken salad here you could at least get the employees to keep their fingers out of it," I say.

He laughs. "Yeah, you would think so" and goes back to conversing with the couple.

Soon Mike brings out a new sandwich. I have finished my dinner but still have time to kill before the concert ends. Since the restaurant is no longer busy enough for me to worry about taking up a seat, I decide to stay and keep reading my book.

"That better?" Mike asks.

"Oh yeah. And this beer is fantastic, pairs nicely with the crispy sweet potato fries."

The fries pair nicely with the beer? Does this guy think he's some kind of foodie? Probably belongs to a local band too. The couple gets up to leave and Mike walks them out of the restaurant.

Hipster guy turns toward me. "What are you reading?"

I am startled because I thought I was invisible. *"Passenger,"* I reply, "It's a book I am reading for the book club I host for my residents at work, but I'm having a hard time getting into it."

"I'm Jack," he says and reaches across the chair with his hand. I notice a few tattoos going up his arm. His hand is warm and strong.

"I'm Jayme," I say, staring into his eyes, shaking his hand just a little too long. I pull back awkwardly and turn back to my Kindle.

"So where do you work?"

Oh, I guess we are going to keep talking then. "I work at The Village."

"That's a nice place. What do you do there?" Wow. The beginning of an actual adult conversation with a stranger. Okay, you can do this, I tell myself. "I'm the activities director."

"That sounds interesting."

Really? *That* sounds interesting?

"So you're hosting a book club? What kind of books do you read?" he asked.

Is he seriously going to talk to me about books?

"Well, we tend to read a lot of historical fiction. Lately almost everything is about World War II, as if that's the only point in history anyone can write about anymore. The residents love the time period, but are kinda tired of it, so we are trying out some new genres. This particular book has time travel. I'm not sure how well it will be received."

"But what kind of books do *you* like to read outside of your book club?"

Whoa there buddy. I just met you, and you're asking me to bear my soul?

I'm telling myself to lie but instead hear myself say, "To be honest, I gravitate towards fantasy and dystopian novels. *Harry Potter* is my all-time favorite, as you can see," I say, blushing again as I point at the *Deathly Hallows* tattoo on my wrist.

What are you doing?! I ask myself. You just met this guy!

"I had a stint with fantasy too, but I really prefer westerns. *Lonesome Dove* is probably my all-time favorite."

Am I dreaming? Maybe the bartender slipped me vodka instead of water.

"If they like historical fiction you might try *World, Chase Me Down* by Andrew Hilleman. It's about Pat Crowe, set in the American frontier. That would give you historical fiction, but not World War II. I really enjoyed it."

His eyes sparkle as he tells me about some of the other books he's read recently.

"Well, I will definitely consider them," I say. I can hardly believe it. I am talking about books to a complete stranger. My skin is tingly and my mind is racing.

"So Jack, where do you work?"

"Oh, I'm a horse trainer at Stormy Ranch."

At this point I'm pretty sure I black out. Am I seriously talking to a man who trains horses for rehabilitation services, *and* loves to read? His ripped jeans, t-shirt, chucks, and tattoos, led me to believe he is just another foodie hipster type. This guys is a *real-life* cowboy! Somebody pinch me.

"Well, that definitely sounds more interesting than leading activities."

Is that all you have to say? God, you're dull, I chastise myself.

"It's hard work, but every day, every horse, is a new and exciting adventure."

Swoon.

"I had better get goin'; have an early start tomorrow. It was nice to meet you Jayme, I hope you enjoy the book." He reaches across the chair. Electricity shoots up my arm as I grasp his hand.

"Thanks again for the suggestion. Have a good night."

He stands up and I notice the graphic on his T-Shirt.
Star Wars! Jack flashes another smile

I can still smell the suede and Old Spice as he saunters out the door. I wonder if I'll see my space cowboy again. Maybe I could be his next new and exciting adventure...

Old Sight

Jennifer McMurrain

Halloween 1998

Angela's friends pulled her by both arms as they entered the frat party. They knew full well that Angela didn't want to go. Finals started Monday and Angela needed to study.

"I'm going back to the dorms," Angela protested.

"No, you're not," said her roommate and best friend, Hallie. "You're already going to graduate Summa Cum Laude. Even if you skip all your midterms and finals, you'd still graduate with honors. In the four years we've gone to Burnberry University together you've gone out with us exactly three times. That's once a year and now we're going to continue that tradition."

"I go out with you two all the time," countered Angela.

"Going out to dinner is not the same as going to a party," said her friend, Wendy. "Come on, show everyone else how fun you are. Besides we're all dressed up and how else are you going to show everyone that awesome fortune teller costume."

"Fine," Angela huffed. "I'll stay one hour, but if I'm

not having fun I'm going back to the dorms."

"Two hours," said Hallie, slipping on her hippie sunglasses to make her cool 70's chick costume complete, "and if you're not having fun, I'll drive you back myself."

"Deal," said Angela as her friends let go of her arms.

"Remember, go in and get your own Solo cup and fill it with soda," instructed Wendy, as she straightened her kitty cat ears. "If anyone asks, you're drinking a Crown and Coke or vodka 7up. Don't drink anything anyone else offers you."

Angela was very thankful her friends weren't drinkers. Wendy's family was very religious and never consumed alcohol, and Hallie had confided to them that she'd gotten so drunk in high school that she'd puked up her toenails and vowed never to drink again. Hallie's metaphoric visual still made Angela's stomach turn.

The girls entered the party that was being held in an old post office. A young man dressed as a cop stood behind the old post office desk and gave them a smile. "I need to see IDs and if you're gonna drink, cover is five dollars for a cup. If you don't want a cup, you can go across the street to the kiddie park, 'cause this here is a drinkin' party."

Hallie slid a twenty and their IDs across the counter. "Three please."

The young man glanced at their IDs and then reached to his side for three red Solo cups and Hallie's change.

"Does the handsome counter boy get a tip?" asked the young man holding up her five dollars in change.

Hallie gave him a sly look and nabbed her change before the boy could react. "Only if he were handsome."

"That's cold," said the boy, laughing as the girls

walked into the party with their cups, "but I'll melt you."

Hallie rolled her eyes. "I bet he's a freshman. They always make the fish work the front."

"He wasn't bad looking," said Angela, feeling a little sorry for the young man.

"No, he wasn't," said Hallie, "but he shouldn't have called himself handsome. Ick."

The girls laughed. The main room of the party was being held in what Angela figured used to be an old mail-sorting room. The sorting equipment was gone, replaced with tables, mismatched chairs and random couches. A ping-pong table was being used for beer pong at one end of the room, while the other was converted into a dance floor. College students dressed in various costumes mingled around, laughing, joking, dancing, and a few couples had even started making out.

The girls filled their cups full of soda and then hurried onto the dance floor. Soon Angela was full of giggles as the girls spun and danced with each other. As the music slowed the girls made their way to an empty avocado green couch.

"Look, there's Ryan," said Hallie. "Oh, my goodness, he's dressed like a hippie. It's like it was meant to be."

"Go talk to him," encouraged Angela, knowing Hallie had had a crush on Ryan for the past two years. "It's now or never."

"Oh, I couldn't," said Hallie.

"Give me you palm," said Angela.

"Here?" Hallie gave Wendy a side glance.

"Yes," said Angela. "It's just palm reading and it totally fits my costume. People will think we're just goofing around."

"It's just," Wendy bit her lip, "you've always been so careful not to tell anyone what you can do."

Angela rolled her eyes. "You guys are sweet, but seriously, I'm dressed as a fortune teller. It's not a big deal. Besides no one is paying any attention to us, now let me give you a reading, or go up to Ryan cold."

Hallie looked over at Ryan and then returned her gaze to Angela, before reaching toward her, palm up.

Angela gently took Hallie's hand and ran her fingers delicately over the lines. She had read a lot of books on palm reading and knew each line and what it stood for, but that wasn't how her gift worked. Her gift was like a blind man reading braille, only as her fingers crossed the lines, she could see images instead of words.

As her hand glided over Hallie's palm, she saw Hallie going up to Ryan and the two striking up a conversation. The two would leave the party early and when they left, Ryan would kiss her and Hallie's heart would be full.

"You need to go talk to him. Now," said Angela letting go of Hallie's hand. "It will end well."

"Are you sure?" Hallie bit her lip.

"The palm doesn't lie," said Angela with a shrug. "But it's your choice."

"Remember that time Angela read your palm and said you'd ace your chem final and then you did," said Wendy. "What's the harm in trying?"

"You're right," said Hallie, standing. "I'm doing it. Wish me luck."

Angela watched as Hallie sauntered over to Ryan. She tapped him gently on the shoulder and when he turned and saw Hallie his smiled widened. They pointed to each other's costumes and laughed. Ryan whispered something into Hallie's ear and she nodded.

"That's the last we'll see of her until it's time to go," said Angela. "I bet she and Ryan will be outside talking all night."

Two girls, one dressed as a seductive mummy and the other a cop in hot pants, approached Wendy and Angela.

"Did we just see you give that girl a palm reading?" asked the mummy.

Angela smiled and pointed to her costume. "I'm just playing the part, you know for fun."

The mummy and cop looked at each other and giggled. "Could you read our palms?"

"For five dollars," Wendy said quickly.

Angela flashed her a look. Wendy shrugged. "What? You have to be able to pay for your crystal ball and tarot cards."

Angela turned back to the girls getting ready to politely decline reading their palms, when the girl dressed as a mummy handed her twenty dollars.

"This is all I have on me," the mummy said, "so how about you give us each a reading for ten dollars apiece?"

"Do it," Wendy whispered.

Angela let out a sigh. She hadn't read for anyone other than her friends.

"Come on," said the cop, "just for fun."

"What will it hurt?" said Wendy.

Angela plastered on a smile. Her mind warned her that she might be going down a rabbit hole with no exit. There was a chance that everyone would think she was a freak if her readings came true or they wouldn't leave her alone asking for more readings. She didn't want to be labeled as the physic weirdo around campus.

With Wendy, the mummy, and cop looking at her, their eyes eager with anticipation, Angela decided to play the part and give them fake readings.

"Okay." This time, she felt a true smile caressing her face, "as long as you guys know I'm totally making this stuff up."

"Of course," said the cop, as the mummy handed Hallie the twenty-dollar bill. "Do me first."

The cop thrust out her hand and Angela took it. She slid her finger down the girl's palm. Flashes of fire and screaming raced through her mind. The heat was unbearable and Angela dropped the girl's hand as she jerked backwards.

"Oh this is going to be good," said the mummy.

"What is it?" asked the cop, looking at her palm as if she could see what Angela had seen.

"Fire," said Angela, her voice weak and her throat feeling raw as if she had walked through the fire herself. "I saw a huge fire and heard people screaming."

The cop rubbed her arms. "She just gave me goosebumps."

"Awesome," said the mummy, thrusting out her hand. "Now do me."

Angela hesitated, her eyes still on the girl dressed as cop. How could she tell her that the premonition had been true? How could she warn this poor girl that she was going to be in a deadly fire? Her mind warned her to play it cool.

"I'm not sure I want to do any more," Angela said weakly.

"Come on," whined the mummy, "I've already paid you. You said yourself it's all fake, right?"

Angela glanced at the cop. The look of worry on the girl's face spoke volumes. Angela had to do something to save her, but the words *freak* and *weirdo* kept running through her head.

Angela gave the mummy a nod and took her hand. Even as her finger hovered above the mummy's palm, Angela's mind was again met with flames, screaming and unbearable heat. People did a morbid dance around her as they flung their blazing arms and legs about, looking for some kind of relief. Angela's chest ached, making it impossible to breathe. She knew the cop and the mummy were going to be in the same fire and the mummy wasn't going to make it out alive. She would die of smoke inhalation.

Angela clamped her hand down on the mummy's hand and forced a deep breath, reminding herself that she wasn't actually in the fire. She needed to see where the fire was going to take place. She had to warn these girls. She closed her eyes and pushed away the heat and flames, forcing herself to find something in the room not ablaze that would tell her where the girls were.

Her mind's eye flashed to an avocado green couch. She had seen that couch before but couldn't quite place where. Then she saw the boy handing out Solo cups. He jumped over the counter, his back on fire and began to roll around on the ground. Her nose wrinkled as she smelled the gas.

Her eyes shot open and she looked down. She was sitting on the avocado green couch. She looked over to the boy handing out cups as he leaned on the counter talking to

WordWeavers

some girl dressed as a hula dancer. Panic ripped through her body.

She grabbed Wendy's hand and traced a finger down her palm and was met with the same images.

"What?" asked the mummy. "You look seriously freaked out. Are you a theatre major or something, because this is over the top? Remember it was supposed to be for fun." She looked to her cop friend. "Let's go, I don't want to hang out with these freaks anymore."

Angela ignored the girl and reached behind her grabbing a boy's hand.

"Hey," he said, trying to jerk it away. Angela was able to read his palm before he did and again saw the flames. She grabbed a random girl's palm next and bit back a scream of terror as she felt the girl's burning flesh.

"We have to get out of here," Angela said as she released the girl's hand. "All of us, there's going to be a fire. We have to go!"

Wendy shook her head. "I don't smell anything."

Angela grabbed Wendy by the shoulders. "When have I been wrong? I see the same thing in every palm I've touched since Wendy's and she went outside."

"Okay," said Wendy, "but how do we get everyone out?"

"Go pull the fire alarm and then get out," said Angela. "I'll get the DJ to make an announcement."

Wendy gave Angela a quick hug before running towards the nearest wall in search of a fire alarm. Angela pushed her way through the crowd toward the DJ.

"I think there's a gas leak," she yelled to the DJ over the loud music. "Everyone needs to get out."

Tea Cozies and Terabytes: People

The DJ shook his head. "I don't smell anything."

A loud alarm bell started to ring through the air and Angela sighed in relief. Wendy had found the fire alarm.

"See, we have to go!" said Angela. She looked around the room and was surprised to find all the people looking at the ceiling or each other as if they'd never heard a fire alarm before. "Tell them!"

The DJ stopped his music and turned on his mic. "I hate to be a bummer, but I'm being told by this fortune teller that there might be a gas leak. So we should all probably go outside until we get the all clear from the authorities. Dump your cups on the way out, if you're smart."

"Thank you," said Angela.

The smell of gas was getting thicker, but the crowd was just casually walking out as if they were leaving class and not trying to evacuate the building before it exploded.

"Move!" yelled Angela from the back of the room. "You have to get out now! Hurry!"

Angela rubbed her palms together in worry. As her fingers grazed her opposite palm she saw what was to come. Ferocious heat engulfed her body as the smell of melting plastic, fabric, and metal assaulted her nose. The pain radiated over her body and then the whole world went black.

Her vision faded as the last person walked out the door. She hurried to follow them, hoping to avoid her own ill-fated vision. As her hand touched to the door, she heard a *whoosh* right before the scream of fire. Ferocious heat engulfed her body as the smell of melting plastic, fabric, and metal assaulted her nose. As the pain radiated over her body, she felt herself flying, but smiled knowing she had saved them all, right before the whole world went black.

New Sight

Jennifer McMurrain

Halloween 2018

Two girls stood in front of the shell of the old post office building that had burnt twenty years earlier during a Halloween Party.

"You have to go in," insisted Emily.

"Do I?" asked Olivia. Her hands trembled and she felt as if she were going to vomit. "A girl died in there."

"You do if you want to be part of our sorority," came a voice from the shadows.

Olivia sighed. She knew that voice, it was Lauren Masters, president of the Chi Chi Sorority, that both Olivia and Emily were pledges for.

"It just seems...," Olivia bit her lip. "... I don't know, like I'm dishonoring her some way. She saved all those people and now she's been reduced to a ghost story and a dare."

Lauren laughed. "You're overthinking this, Olivia. You walk in, you stay there for half an hour, you walk out. It's that easy."

"Can't I just eat 20 tacos in a row like Emily did?"

asked Olivia. "You can even put hot sauce on them."

Lauren shook her head. "You pulled from the jar. This is your task."

Other girls from the Chi Chi Sorority started to show up. All wanting to know if Olivia would go through with staying half an hour in the scariest place in town.

Emily turned Olivia to face her. "A: It's just a burnt-out building. B: That girl, she's not here. I'm sure she got a parade in the afterlife for saving all those people. So why would she be haunting this awful place? C: You do not want to eat 20 tacos, remember how I barfed most of the night? Now imagine that with hot sauce." Emily smiled and Olivia couldn't help but smile back. "This is easy. Mind over matter and then we can both be Chi Chi. I'm going to be right here the whole time."

Emily was right, it was just an old building and ghosts weren't real. Anything she saw in the old building would be her imagination or a trick put on by the sorority sisters.

"It's midnight," said Lauren, tapping her smart watch. "Enter or quit."

Olivia took a deep breath. "Okay, I'm going in."

"Get rid of your phone," said Lauren. "You can't have any light. We'll call you out in half an hour. Chi promise."

Olivia handed her cell phone to Emily. Taking another deep breath, Olivia walked toward the old post office. As she got closer she could smell the rot and old burn of the building. It wasn't highly unpleasant and vaguely reminded her of her grandfather's old pipe.

She ducked under the caution tape that hung haphazardly over the doorway. The building hadn't been touched since the fire and the doors had been completely blown off the post office. She stood in the doorway and turned around. Technically she was in the building.

"That's not going to cut it," hollered Lauren. "You have to go all the way in. Where we can't see you and you can't see us."

Olivia sighed. A part of her knew it wouldn't be that easy, but she had to try. She turned and walked further into the building. The floor was a solid cement slab, so falling through wasn't going to be an issue, instead Olivia worried about snagging her leg on a jagged board or stepping on a nail. The last thing she wanted was to spend the night in the ER waiting to get a tetanus shot.

She walked past what looked to be the old post office's main desk and made her way to what she believed was the mail-sorting room. There were a couple of burned out couches and chairs on one side, what looked to be an old game table on the other, and a platform with an empty space in front, probably for dancing.

Olivia had to admit, it would be the perfect place for a party. Open with plenty of room, not like the frat parties she had been too that were old houses stuffed to the gills with people and booze. She stood in the middle of the room and tried to imagine what it must have been like before the fire. Just a typical Halloween party, with drinks and dancing, and probably some making out on the couches and dark corners.

"Well, this isn't so bad," she said to the quiet room. She expected there to be creaks and squeaks throughout the old building that she would be jumping at every sound. "Now, I wait."

She walked over to the arm of one of the couches and leaned against it. She wished she had her cell phone so she'd at least have something to do while she waited.

"The party ended a long time ago," came a voice from the back room. "You shouldn't be here."

Olivia let out a scream as she stumbled to her feet and turned. Then she laughed as she saw a girl a little older than her standing in the back doorway. She wore an old-fashioned broom skirt, peasant shirt, and had gold chains hanging from her neck and across her forehead. She looked very much like a stereotypical fortune teller.

"Oh my gosh," laughed Olivia. "You got me. I knew y'all would be up to something and I should have been expecting it."

The girl shook her head. "Expecting what?"

"That someone would come in and scare me," said Olivia. "I mean it's not much of a challenge if I just sit in the dark for half an hour. I bet Lauren would like nothing more than for me to wet my pants and run out crying. Not going to happen."

The girl walked closer, her brows furrowed. "Who is Lauren? Did she not get out? I thought I got everyone out."

Olivia shook her head. "I hope you're not a drama major, because your acting is terrible."

"Who are you?" asked the girl as she stepped even closer.

Olivia thrust out her hand. "I'm Olivia, you know the girl you're supposed to scare out of here so I don't pass the Chi Chi's test."

"What is a Chi Chi?" asked the girl.

"The sorority," said Olivia with a sigh. "Really, this act is getting old. How about we just have a conversation until my time is up. It's so boring in here. I'll come out saying I thought I saw a ghost and you can put this on your resume or whatever."

"Your time is up?" asked the girl with a tilt of her head. "Did I give you a reading? Is that something I told you?"

"Fine," said Olivia, with a shrug, "you're committed to your role, but I'm done here. I'd rather be bored than play this game."

She leaned back against the arm of the couch with her back to the girl. She couldn't believe she had been scared to enter the old building or that Lauren had given her such a lame excuse of a ghost. Emily was right, this was going to be a lot easier than eating 20 twenty tacos in one sitting.

The girl stepped around to face Olivia. "You mentioned conversation?"

"Sure," said Olivia, "beats doing nothing."

"What year is it?" asked the girl.

Olivia rolled her eyes. Apparently the game was still on. "2018."

"What day?"

"October 31st, Halloween."

"No," said the girl. "You shouldn't be here. Not today, not any day, but especially not on the anniversary."

"Don't worry I'll be leaving in about twenty minutes," said Olivia. "Well, I think, I have no concept of time without my phone."

"You have to leave," urged the girl. "They'll come out. They always do, and on this anniversary there will be so many. It's so awful. They rip at my body as if wanting a part of my soul. They'll do it to you too."

"Okay, so this story is getting better," said Olivia.

"Who will rip out my soul?"

"The shadows," whispered the girl, "the gas leak was no accident and they are angry at me because they wanted all those souls. I cheated death and they are angry. This is the year they take me, my soul for the twenty that should have been lost in the fire."

"So this is a riddle?" asked Olivia. "Because, you died and they could've taken you a long time ago, so you didn't cheat death ... and I'm pretty sure that's not how death works."

"I upset the balance," said the girl looking around the room. "Every year on this date, they come and rip at me, trying to drag me down. It hurts. It burns, but this is the year they collect their debt. You aren't safe. They will take you as a bonus. You have to leave."

"I'm not going anywhere," said Olivia. "Not until they call me out. I'm not falling for this ghost story."

A soft moan floated on the air.

"They're coming," said the girl. "You have to go or you will die. Let them take me. I'm who they want. I'm the one who ruined their plans."

Olivia felt the hairs on the back of her neck rise. The moans grew louder and more abundant, as Olivia stood firmly on her feet. The shadows of the room seemed to move on their own. There was no light, not even moonlight shining through the broken parts of the roof ... no reason for the shadows to move.

"It's just a trick," Olivia told herself. "Just something to get me to run out of here."

"No," said the girl. "You have to leave. You haven't much time."

Olivia shook her head as the moving shadows took human form, but remained pitch black, aside from their fiery red eyes. Try as she might she couldn't figure out how the Chi Chi's were making the shadows move so fluently. Fear raced through her body as she fought the urge to flee.

"Angela, did you bring us a present?" hissed one of the shadows.

"She does look tasty," hissed another.

"How is this happening?" Olivia asked Angela, her hands shaking.

"Leave her alone," shouted Angela, pulling Olivia behind her in a protective position. "It is me you're after. She has more time. I have seen it."

"You read her palm did you?" asked the shadow. "Maybe you should read it again? Our fates change with our choices and she has made a very poor one by coming here tonight."

"I will," said Angela. "I'll read it right here, but you have to promise if the fates say she lives, you let her walk out. You can't take a soul that isn't yours. Tonight you are due one soul, mine. Do we have a deal?"

Olivia could've sworn she saw the shadow shrug.

"Makes no difference to us. Her time will come. Time always comes. Now tell us, fortune teller, is her time tonight?"

"And do not lie," hissed another shadow. "We can taste the lies on the air."

Angela turned and faced Olivia. "Twenty years ago I was able to save twenty people. If the reading says you have more time you have to leave. If you don't, they will take you and that sacrifice I made twenty years ago will be for nothing. I know this doesn't seem real. I understand you were sent in here on some kind of dare. But can't you feel it? Can't you feel the heaviness of death?"

Olivia nodded. Even as her mind raced to find an explanation, in her heart she knew it was all too real. The air was thick with dread and her head buzzed and felt compressed. It was nothing she had ever felt before, but the energy of the room was dark and she wanted nothing more than to leave. Even if that meant she would disappoint Emily by not being a Chi Chi.

"Give me your palm," ordered Angela. "They're right. I can't lie, so if this is bad news, just stay behind me." Angela looked down. "And I'm sorry you're paying for my sacrifice."

"Enough with the talking," growled a shadow. "I'm hungry."

"Are you going to Hell?" asked Olivia, unable to believe the words had come out of her mouth. "You saved all those people." She swallowed hard. "Will I go to Hell if this reading says it's my time?"

"I don't know," said Angela softly.

"Get on with it!" snarled the shadow closest to them and Olivia felt his anger like waves of heat coming off a bonfire.

Olivia gave Angela her palm. Angela gently slid her finger down the lines. She was quiet for a moment, a look of confusion on her face.

"I have to do it again," stated Angela. "The message wasn't clear."

Olivia felt her heart leap into her throat and bit back a scream. She didn't like the look on Angela's face. Tears started to fall on Olivia's cheeks as she thought of how she had blown her mother off on the phone earlier, eager to get to the Halloween festivities on campus. She hadn't even said I love you. Just a quick hang up. Her lip started to tremble, and she knew she was close to sobbing. She wasn't ready to die. She needed to see her family again.

Angela gave her hand a reassuring squeeze. "It'll be okay."

Angela again swiped her finger down the length of Olivia's palm. This time instead of fear a sense of peace and warmth flooded her body.

"It is not her time," announced Angela.

The shadows groaned in disappointment as Angela dropped Olivia's hand.

Pick up Angela's hand and slid your finger across her palm, came a soft voice in Olivia's ear.

The voice was comforting like a caring grandmother and made any residing fear Olivia felt melt like warm honey. She did as she was told and grabbed Angela's hand. She was surprised to find it as solid as her own.

Angela looked at her in confusion as Olivia slid her finger down Angela's palm.

A vision floated through Olivia's mind, she saw not the shadows taking Angela, but a bright white light. Inside the light were star-like twinkles and Olivia could feel the love surrounding Angela as the shadows shrunk away.

"It's time," said a shadow. It turned toward Olivia. "You had better scurry off."

"No!" called out Olivia. "I have seen it. It is Angela's time, but you don't get her."

"We are owed this soul!" screeched a shadow. "It is

ours."

"I saw it," said Olivia, "and you know I can't lie. It is a white light that takes Angela, not shadows."

Just as she said it, a white light flashed through the ceiling and just like in her vision, she could feel the love and see the star-like twinkles. Angela took a step towards it as the shadows screamed, causing the earth to tremble in anger as they shrank away.

"It's so beautiful," said Angela and Olivia could see the tears in her eyes. "Thank you."

Angela floated into the white light and was gone. Olivia blinked hard as the world went dark and tried to adjust her sight. She searched for the shadow creatures, wondering if they would come for her anyway now that Angela was gone. After all they were still owed a soul.

"Olivia!" came a shout from the hallway and Olivia knew it was Emily. The shadows stirred at the entrance of a new soul entering the building causing Olivia to run to her friend.

Emily wrapped her up in a hug. "Did you feel the earthquake? I was so scared for you. We all are."

Olivia turned to see Lauren and the other Chi's standing, ready to help if needed.

"I'm okay, but we have to get out of here," said Olivia, as a soft moan caressed the air just as it had done before. "It isn't safe."

"You're right," said Lauren, "everyone out. There's no telling what the earthquake did to what's left of the building. Everyone out!"

They rushed out and Olivia felt a sense of relief wash over her as she exited the door. Emily gave her another hug.

"I was so worried."

"That's it," said Lauren. "We're taking this old building challenge out of the jar. I don't want anyone getting hurt. That's not what this sorority is about."

Olivia let out another sigh of relief. With Lauren's proclamation, that meant future Chi Chi wouldn't become victims to the shadows and their search for the final soul.

As Emily handed Olivia her cell phone, Olivia's finger brushed against Emily's palm. Visions flashed in her mind of her, Emily, and Lauren becoming good friends, their college careers being tough, but successful, and she and Emily watching as the old post office was torn down, leaving the shadows crying over the final soul they would never retrieve.

Show and Tell Daddy

Cindy Molder

My Daddy (yes, middle-aged Southern women still call their fathers Daddy) didn't tell me he loved me until I was fifty years old. I am not sure why those three words escaped him for so long. But I'll always remember the day he finally said it.

He had been released from the hospital after open-heart surgery and I called to check on him. Our post-hospital chat was different. Usually, Daddy wasn't much for small talk or long phone calls, but during this lengthy conversation, he talked a little about "dyin" and he laughed a lot about having a pig heart valve in his chest.

"You know I had a choice between a cadaver valve or a pig heart valve. I chose the dad-gum pig. I love ham and I don't much care for dead people," he teased.

I giggled like girls do when their daddies are silly, "If you grow a snout then we know the pig graft took just fine."

As an adult, when I ended a phone call with him, I always said, "I love you, Daddy." His response had always been, "See ya."

This time when I was about to hang up it was different,

Tea Cozies and Terabytes: People

I said, "I better let you go so you can rest. I'm glad you're back to your old self. I'll call you later this week. Take care, okay? I love you, Daddy."

I waited but didn't hear the quick, "See ya."

Instead his voice broke and quivered. I heard the words I had longed to hear my entire life, "I love y'all, too."

To say "I love you" singular would have meant only me. That would have been too hard, too intimate. When he said "y'all" he covered the deeper meaning of plural. With one contraction, he lumped together the whole bunch of us, including me, the one I had married and those I had borne.

He didn't say another word as he quickly hung up the phone.

I don't remember a hug from Daddy until I left home to move five hundred miles away. He squeezed the tar out of me that day and he lingered long with two-handed soft pats on my back. He whispered in my ear, "You always have a home here. Don't you forget who you are girl." When he loosened the embrace, I looked over his shoulder and watched as my momma's eyes filled with tears. That was a first, too. I'm not sure if she was sad to see me go or touched to see Daddy hug his firstborn.

Even though we weren't a huggy, kissy, verbally-affirming family, I always knew I was loved. The man who had difficulty saying it, showed it to me all the time.

After a long day working in the auto parts store, he would come home ready to play with his own children, as well as those who didn't have a male parent in the home. He was the stand-in father to all the kids in the neighborhood. While momma fixed supper, he kept us busy with outdoor games.

He taught us to play baseball and softball. "Drop your tailgate" meant a ground ball is coming your way. "Pop fly" was code for look up, keep your eyes on the ball and use two hands so the ball won't pop out of your glove. We had to learn every position on the team. As he coached he would remind us, "You can't just play pitcher or hind-catcher, there's a big field to cover."

He let us trample down the backyard grass to run the bases. As a grown man, he could run like a jack rabbit and he never cut us any slack. He always tagged us out as we rounded third base headed for home.

Without a lot of disposable income, Daddy found a way to expose us to everything. We went to the mountains, beach, theme parks, rodeos, museums, and bookstores. We went as far as the family Chevy could safely take us on a seven-day adventure or a weekend getaway. He loved the Atlanta Braves and a doubleheader in the hot Georgia sun was better than a trip to Disneyland. As we baked in the summer heat of the Deep South, he bought us Pepsi-Colas until his money ran out.

I loved college basketball as a young girl and he managed to get his hands on two tickets to see Vanderbilt and the University of Tennessee play. On a weeknight, just Daddy and I drove to Nashville to see the game. I felt like a queen even though he never told me I was one. Someone at the game spilled a drink on my new sweatshirt and I cried; he dried me off and winked at me, "It's okay Sis." His words let me know all was right with the world and that night it was.

We weren't a big church-going family and when we went, we were the ones who were always late. With three young children, it took a lot for us to get ready to go anywhere. One Sunday morning, we were behind schedule of course, and we were driving down the main county highway headed to our rural Methodist church. We passed an elderly couple who were parked on the side of the road with their hood up, steam escaping in the front. Daddy put on the brakes, pulled to the shoulder of the road and backed up to the older couple's car.

My momma crossed her arms and didn't say a word. This wasn't the first time he stopped to help a stranded traveler. I knew to keep my mouth shut. I was the oldest after all.

My brother blew his breath in disgust and my baby sister, the brave one, spoke up with a whine, "Daddy, we are going to be late to church again."

I will never forget the look on his face as he turned around and gave us all the evil eye, "Don't you think helping these old folks is more important than getting to church on time? Now you hush up."

She dropped her head and said, "Yes, sir."

He kept a tool box in the trunk for such occasions and he knew how to fix anything. With black electrical tape, he wrapped the broken-down car's radiator hose that had a hole in it. He took an empty bottle he found in the grass and walked down to a creek to get water to add to the radiator. It took several trips to get enough to refill the tank. By the time the stranded motorist's car was repaired, Daddy's church clothes were wringing wet with sweat and we had missed all of the church service. The older couple went on their way. We went home. He never once complained.

It was my first high school homecoming and everyone

wore long dresses to the dance. I didn't have much money of my own, only a little I made babysitting, but that didn't keep me from shopping for the perfect outfit and I found it, a simple black and white dress, three times the price I could afford. The store clerk offered layaway but I knew I couldn't earn enough before the event.

I thought I was going to have to break my date with the cute football player that had asked me because I didn't have anything to wear. I tried to borrow a dress but I was small for my age and none of my friends' dresses fit me.

Two weeks before homecoming, I came home late on a Friday afternoon. I thought it odd that Daddy was already there. I walked down the hall to my bedroom and hanging on the door was the beautiful long dress, the very one I had picked out a few weeks before.

Daddy walked past my room and winked, "I wonder how that got there."

I wanted to run and hug him and say, "I love you." But all I could say was, "Did you do that? Thank you, Daddy." I learned later he called the store where I found the dress and told the clerk, his little girl saw a dress she wanted and he would like to put it on layaway.

I'm sure he had to sacrifice something in the budget to buy that dress but whatever he did without wasn't to the detriment of his family.

Some folks say a young woman's self-image, good or bad, is a result of her relationship with her father. In my life, I would agree. Times are different now and today most fathers show affection openly and tell their children they are loved many times a day. But I don't feel short- changed in the least. He showed me he loved me when I was younger and now that I am older, he tells me. I am a lucky girl because I have both, a "Show" and a "Tell" Daddy.

Choice

Cindy Molder

Last fall my husband and I decided to visit my parents for Thanksgiving. It had been years since we traveled on a holiday and my mother seemed pleased that we were coming. My mother was quick to make sure we understood, "Now I don't cook a big meal for the family anymore. If you don't mind, you all can join us for a late Thanksgiving dinner at a restaurant. We can have dessert after we get back home. I will make your favorite Italian Cream Cake. How does that sound?"

I was quick to reassure her, "Momma you know we don't care about eating a huge meal. Going to a restaurant is fine with us. We want to spend our time with you and Daddy, not overeating on turkey and dressing." I think she was relieved.

We arrived at their home, the same home where I had grown up and where they had lived for fifty-five years. As we greeted each other with warm hugs and aging faces, the passing of time had become more evident. Like other times we had visited, we noticed their new wrinkles and I'm sure they did ours.

Tea Cozies and Terabytes: People

The first place I've always headed when I got home was to Momma's kitchen. She liked to follow me and go over the list of menus that she had posted on the refrigerator door. The list usually included all the dishes she planned on cooking while we were home.

But this time was different. When I entered the kitchen, the list was there but she wasn't behind me. I heard her say from the living room, "Don't mind me, I'm going to rest a few more minutes before we leave for the restaurant. There's sweet tea on the counter."

I picked up the old brown Tupperware jug full of still warm fresh brewed tea after I had filled my glass with ice. I poured slowly and when the warm liquid flowed over the ice, it crackled right on cue. It's a southern thing, we never refrigerate our tea, and it tastes better that way. It was usually finished in a day's time so there were never any leftovers.

I was glad she was resting and I could tell she was slowing down as she aged. I took advantage of the few minutes alone in the cozy kitchen. Her kitchen window was sparkling clean and her white eyelet curtains were crisply pressed. I leaned against the enamel sink that was in front of the window and looked out at the back yard where I had played as a child. The old swing set was still there. I heard all those giggles and squeals of cousins and siblings as we played outside. The oak and hickory trees were so big, when did they get so big? I felt the tears fill my eyes. Time flies and things have changed.

As I turned to the left, I ran my hand across the kitchen counter. The turquoise Formica tops were the original ones from 1964. Yep, still spotless and in excellent condition.

Her kitchen was immaculate. I looked at the few cabinets and drawers around the wall, and for some reason I counted them. Two cupboards held plates and glasses, two more contained casserole dishes and plastic ware, a single one in the corner held dry goods, another above the stove hid the canned goods, and two below held cookware and baking pans. She only had three drawers in the whole kitchen, one for silverware, one for cooking utensils, and one for her kitchen towels. I recounted twice and was amazed by so little storage space. Where had I been? Why had I never noticed? How had she survived for fifty-five years in that tiny kitchen? How on earth had she cooked large meals for a family of five and, many times, neighbors and extended family?

I heard her walk in behind me. "Sis, did you find the tea?"

"Yes ma'am, right where it always was, thanks for making it. Your tea is the best," I answered.

"Just wanted to let you know we will leave for the restaurant in about fifteen minutes," she said.

"Momma, I was looking around in here and after all these years, I have never noticed how few cabinets you have to use."

"There's not a lot of storage or work space in here, but I made do," she remarked.

"Did you and Daddy ever think about adding on or remodeling?" I questioned.

"We did a couple of times, thought about adding an island and changing the counter tops and floor," she explained.

I looked down at the linoleum floor. "That's not the

original floor is it? I remember the original floor had a smaller pattern."

She teased, "I can't believe you remember that original floor, and you haven't noticed the cabinets before now. That real bad winter in 1982 caused the water pipes to burst in the garage, and it flooded the living room and kitchen. We replaced it then. It's still good so we haven't had to change it. No reason to now at our age."

I felt a stab in my heart. I knew we were talking about more than the floor, we were talking about the passing of time. It was one of those rare mother-daughter moments. She knew I was full of questions and she stood silent and pondered what was discussed. Silence loomed in the room and right beside it was another question I had to ask.

"Momma, is your strong character due to how you were raised or is it part of the older generation? I mean you made it work and not one time did I hear you complain. I never heard you put pressure on Daddy to spend money that you didn't have for a new kitchen. How did you stay content?" I prodded her for more information and I wanted to know how she had been uniquely satisfied with her life.

"Honey, there's really no secret to contentment. I didn't ever have a big fancy kitchen so I never knew any different. I made it work and lacked nothing. I learned a long time ago, contentment is a choice, and you won't miss what you never had."

I knew then - I still had a lot to learn from my momma.

Wednesday Morning

Eloise Peacock

Born and raised in Tulsa, I loved all the opportunities to be with people: the world-class Gathering Place, restaurants, theaters, music of all kinds, art galleries — everything a divorced woman like me (late thirties and holding) could want. I had fun girls-nights-out, and occasionally I'd meet a nice man and we'd have two or three dates, but nothing really clicked.

So when the company I worked for offered me a position in Bartlesville, a small city an hour north, I went for it. Tulsa traffic was starting to annoy me, and I told myself that a smaller city would offer better prospects for meeting a man I could settle down with. I was wrong: the traffic was lighter, but after a year I hadn't met even one interesting and available man.

I was too old to socialize with my young professional co-workers, and men my age were happily married. I went to barbeques, weddings, baby showers — and felt like a maiden aunt. Some weekends I'd drive into Tulsa and see friends, but I no longer felt at home there.

Nights were lonely, even though I'd taken in a sweet stray cat, a fluffy orange tabby. I named him George Burns and told him he was the man of the house — a charming two-bedroom house I rented for less than I'd paid for my small high-rise Tulsa apartment. I had fun furnishing my home, finding shabby-chic décor in nearby antique stores and quirky thrift shops.

My favorite shop was called Wednesday Morning, and it was open only on — you guessed it — Wednesday mornings. My supervisor was also a fan, and we took early lunch breaks on alternate weeks so we could browse for bargains.

One morning I was hunting the collectibles I had started to crave soon after my move: turtles. China turtles, glass, clay, carved wood; I already had at least a dozen. I spotted a tiny white porcelain turtle on a crowded shelf and reached for it just as someone else did. Our hands touched and we both jerked back as if we'd touched a hot stove.

I looked up into the warm brown eyes of a broad-shouldered, denim-clad man, and he smiled down at me.

"You were first," he said. "You can have it."

"That's ... nice of you. I ... I really like it." I surprised myself by blurting, "You see, I've developed a fondness for turtles. They're silly, but I started collecting them right after I moved here, and I ..." I couldn't think of anything else to say. He was attractive and mature, his chestnut brown hair showing a bit of gray at the temples.

His smile broadened, and he said, "Turtles definitely aren't 'silly'."

When he picked up the little figurine and handed it to me I glanced down to see if he wore a wedding ring. He didn't.

He said, "I thought you might be Indian, Turtle Clan. Turtle is brave, loyal, extremely stubborn. And she ultimately reaches her goals."

"Turtle Clan?" I repeated, feeling flustered. "I don't know what you mean. I just ... like turtles." I added, "And I'm not Indian. I mean Native American."

"Both terms are acceptable."
"Oh. Do I look Indian?" My cheeks started to feel uncomfortably hot.

"How do Indians look?"

"I ... I don't know." After an awkward pause I said, "I guess I'll go pay for my turtle." But my feet didn't want to move.

He said, "I'm part Indian."

"Oh ... Is that why you wanted the turtle? You're in the turtle clan?"

"No. I'm Cherokee. We have seven clans, but no turtles."

He grinned. I started to feel annoyed, like he was teasing me, giving me a hard time about political correctness, or ... I realized he was actually flirting! It had been so long since someone had flirted with me, I thought it was a lost art.

"You recently moved here?" he asked.

I nodded. "From Tulsa."

"I'm surprised you don't know about clans."

"Well, they don't teach much about them in schools," I said, defensively. "I know some history, but nothing about specific clans."

"Actually, the local college has an Indian culture course on public television, and I'm a frequent guest lecturer." He took the turtle from my hand, and this time when we touched our fingers brushed lightly, and I felt a definite tingle.

He continued, "You started collecting them after moving here?"

I nodded.

"You're perhaps attracted to turtle because she is connected to the earth, and carries her security — her home — with her."

"Interesting," I said. "How can I find out when you ... um ... lecture?"

"I have an idea. How about going for coffee, and I'll tell you all about clans." His sincere smile held promise. "There's a lot to learn."

The tingle I'd felt turned into a warm glow, and I knew I'd enjoy learning more about Indian lore, and this particular man.

Frank's Five Hundred MPH Mouse

R. D. Sadok

After I buckled myself into my seat on the plane, I pulled Uncle Frank's letter from my pocket and read it again. "Sam, you're a hotshot journalist now, so humor me. I just might have something noteworthy for you to report. Come and see. I'll be watching for you at my front gate."

Uncle Frank was the ultimate nerd. At least that was how my dad described his brother. Science and math had always been Frank's thing – so much so, he'd never settled down and had a family. Dad said none of the girls in high school would have anything to do with Frank because he was too weird. Nevertheless, when I was a boy, I liked Uncle Frank and looked forward to his visits. What others called his wild-eyed look, I saw as playful and fun-loving. We'd go on walks and he'd tell me stories about his heroes of science. There were Rutherford, the father of nuclear physics, Maxwell, who defined electromagnetism, and of course Einstein, his relativity and his famous formula: $E = Mc^2$.

I loved listening to Uncle Frank's stories because he told them with such passion. During my high school years,

Uncle would call me and spend hours on the phone discussing the intricacies of the new math he was developing, explaining it dealt with the fabric of space. I listened politely, but it was all Greek to me. I suppose when he realized the stratospheric altitude by which it was all sailing over my head, he concluded that language and arts were more my thing than math and science.

Despite my majoring in journalism, the link we'd established during my childhood held fast, and we stayed in touch. I learned of his frustration and deep disappointment when his submissions to scientific journals, all of which he felt were of earth-shaking importance, kept being rejected. He told me the dolts simply didn't have the capacity to understand his math.

Up until four years ago, Uncle Frank was a physics professor at the Sedgwitz University. That was before he made national news by winning a humongous, nationwide lottery. The take-home after taxes was over a hundred million.

Uncle Frank wrote that he was retiring from his University professorship and was finally free to pursue his research.

Then Uncle Frank disappeared.

Until I received the letter I now held in my hand, I hadn't heard a word from Uncle Frank in four years, nor had anyone else I knew.

* * *

After glancing at the puffy white clouds ten thousand feet below, I leaned back in my seat, shut my eyes and allowed my thoughts to drift back to a time two years earlier. Because Uncle had stopped communicating, I feared he'd fallen victim to foul play. Maybe someone had stolen his fortune. I wondered if he still alive. I traveled to Sedgwitz, hoping to finding out.

In all honesty, investigating my uncle's disappearance was partially motivated by my hope for selling a good story. I had recently launched my career as freelance journalist and needed funds. Back then, the only Sedgwitz address I had was a post office box, so I hoped to learn his street address from someone at the university.

When I first entered the administration building lobby, an obnoxious flyer on the bulletin board grabbed my attention. Someone had blown up a photo of Uncle Frank and drawn in long, frizzy hair, a twirly mustache and a pointy goatee. Beneath they had spelled out 'Dr. Franklyn N. Steinberg', but had scratched out the 'lyn' and the 'berg'.

I ripped the flyer off the bulletin board, wadded it up and shoved it in my pocket. Why would such a disrespectful blurb of a former professor be displayed in the lobby of the university's administrative building?

Someone tapped me on the shoulder. I turned to see a short, balding man looking at me with piercing brown eyes through his wire rim glasses. "Sir, do you always make a practice of ripping information off of public bulletin boards?"

I unwadded the graffiti from my pocket, held it his face, and asked, "Does Sedgwitz U. always post insulting materials about its former professors?"

The bald man's features softened. "Oh, I tore one of those down this morning myself. The students seem to have an unending supply of those things." He took a step back and raised his brow. "What is your interest in the matter?"

"My name is Sam Steinberg. Dr. Franklyn Steinberg is my uncle. I haven't heard from him in a while, so I came to Sedgwitz, hoping to get in touch with him. Actually, I'm a bit concerned."

The man nodded. "I'm Edgar Williamson, the administrative head of the Physics Department. Please follow me to my office and I'll fill you in."

Minutes later Williamson leaned back in his stuffed leather chair and gazed at me. "After Professor Steinberg won the lottery, he retired, bought the mansion on the hill west of town and erected a high privacy fence around the property. Apparently, he's become a recluse because no one I know has seen or heard from him since."

Williamson continued. "We all knew how angry he'd become over being repeatedly rebuffed by his peers, so after his lottery windfall, his retirement didn't really surprise anyone." He sighed and rubbed his chin. "His disappearance from view and some of the happenings since have been fodder for the rumor mill in this small university town."

"Happenings? What sort of happenings?" I asked.

"Well, for one, he converted his mansion on the hill into a fort. The fence I mentioned has cameras mounted on it that would do justice to a maximum-security prison."

"Why in the world? Umm... You think he's still pursuing his research and wants to keep it secret?"

"That's the town's speculation. Exactly what he's doing, no one knows, but theories abound, some quite wild. He worked out a deal with the electric utility company to equip his property with a substation. I can't imagine what his monthly electric bills must be, or why he needs to consume so much power, but he must be working on something up there. Hints are the frequent power flickers here in town. Only last week, one was accompanied by a bright flash and a loud boom from his hilltop. The latest rumor is that he's generating lightning in his basement."

I shook my head. "In all this time, you say no one in town has seen him? If nothing else, he's got to come down from his hill to buy groceries, right?"

"He's got an employee for that. An autistic man known as Sparky runs his errands. Sparky's so laser focused, he talks to no one and never answers anyone's questions. Maybe he's a savant and can understand the professor's math." Williamson scowled. "No one else can."

"Is there some way I can get in touch with my uncle? A phone number maybe?"

"If he has a phone, I don't know anyone who has his number. Like I said, he's totally isolated himself." Williamson shook his head. "Honestly, I fear for the man's sanity."

"You think this autistic man would take me to see him?"

"Sometimes that strange man isn't seen around town for weeks. Even if you hung around town long enough to run into him, I doubt you'd even get him to look at you, much less get any information from him."

I sighed, stood up, and thanked Williamson for taking time to talk to me.

"One more thing," Williamson said when I was at door. "He's bought a lot of tungsten."

"Tungsten?"

"Yeah, tons of it. Some in town know the man who

delivered it, but no one has the slightest idea what your uncle is doing with it."

Before I left, Williamson gave me directions to Frank's place. On my way up the hill west of town, I saw a few more of the disgusting flyers I'd ripped off the university's bulletin board. Some were tacked on telephone poles. One was stuck on Frank's massive front gate, a fifteen-foot high Gothic structure of iron. Rather than a prison, the barrier surrounding Uncle's hilltop brought to mind a medieval castle. Only thing missing was the moat. Williamson said that somewhere beyond that forbidding gate and the trees behind it was Uncle Frank's mansion, but how was I to let him know I was here? I honked. That didn't help. I spotted a camera on top of a pillar next to the gate, stood in front of it, waved my arms and shouted. Nothing. I even bruised my knuckles banging them against that humongous iron gate. Nada. Half an hour later, feeling dejected, I got back in the car and drove back to town. That evening I spoke with a few others on campus and around town. Their stories all confirmed what I'd learned from Williamson: Uncle Frank was unreachable. The next day, feeling disappointed and more concerned than ever, I booked a flight back home.

* * *

When the plane bumped down on the runway in Sedgwitz, I snapped out of my reverie. That was then. This was now. The difference this time was Uncle Frank had invited me. Twenty minutes later, I sat in my rental car in front of Uncle Frank's enormous gate. A camera on top swiveled and peered down at me. Then, with an ear-piercing squeal, the massive structure slowly swung open. I drove through. To my discomfort, the huge gate closed behind me. I cautiously proceeded up the winding, thousand-foot, tree-lined drive until it opened into a large, circular pavement. On a pedestal in its center was a fearsome, ruby-eyed, twelve-foot-tall, bronze dragon. Beyond was Uncle's huge mansion. Images of the Franklin N. Steinberg flyer zinged through my mind as I let myself out of the car. Though it was a warm day, a chill tickled its way down my spine. With goose bumps, I approached the massive oak entry door with its over-sized, lion-faced knocker.

Before I lifted the knocker, the hinges squeaked and the door slowly swung open. I froze on the spot.

A man with stringy black hair and a slightly deformed back stared at me with enormous eyes. Sparky, I presumed. Without a word he nodded, slowly turned and walked into the bowels of house. I took a deep breath, clenched my teeth, stepped over the threshold and followed. I could hear my pulse beating in my temples. He led me down the front hallway and through a labyrinth of rooms and more hallways. A large black cat scampered out of the way and ran ahead. Finally, we arrived at a large study.

Uncle Frank sat in a high-backed, stuffed leather chair, tenderly stroking the black cat now sitting in his lap. "Down, Tom," he said, "I know you miss your little buddy but you'll be okay."

After the cat scampered off, Uncle looked up at me and smiled. "Sam, it is so good to see you." He stood and extended his hand.

"Good to see you, too, Uncle Frank." I shook his hand and sighed with relief. Uncle wore Dockers and a Polo shirt,

Tea Cozies and Terabytes: People

was clean-shaven, and had short, neatly combed hair. He looked like a guy I'd meet on a golf course, not in a medieval castle.

With a swing of his hand he offered me a seat and turned to the large-eyed man I'd met at the door. "Spencer, would you please bring us some tea?"

The man nodded and marched off as though on a mission.

"The townsfolk know him as Sparky," Uncle said, "a nickname he picked up in his youth, but in respect for the man who has faithfully served me, I refer to him as Spencer, his given name."

Spencer soon returned with two glasses of iced tea on a silver tray. While sipping our tea, I brought Uncle up to speed on family happenings, and Uncle told me how he'd taken Spencer under his wing. He explained how he had brought purpose and joy into the man's life after he had been shunned, beaten down and rejected for many years. I saw the connection between my uncle's empathy for Spencer and the pain of rejection he had personally experienced in his professional life, rejection that even went back to his high school years when he was labeled weird and couldn't make any headway with the girls.

"Uncle, the townspeople say you've become a recluse. It concerned me when I heard that you had isolated yourself up here."

"Ah, but I've only isolated myself from the naysayers at the university and of this community. Instead, with the Internet at my disposal, I have been in good company with Newton, Rutherford, Maxwell, Einstein, Hawkings, Jesus and his apostles." A gleam came to his eye. "They've taught me much and have inspired me greatly."

"Men of both science and religion, Uncle?" I asked, thinking the two were a bit at odds with one another.

"I was seeking wisdom and truth from every worthy source, not only from the creation but its creator." Frank made a grand sweep with his hand. "You really think all this just happened by chance?"

"Um." I shifted in my chair, realizing the *this* he referred to wasn't his mansion but the entirety of existence. "Uncle, in your note you said you wanted to show me something that I could report in my capacity as a journalist. Have you made some sort of breakthrough?"

Frank smiled. "Ah, yes." He stood from his chair, pulled a small tin from his pocket and said, "I think it would be a good idea for you to take one of these." He opened the lid revealing several white pills.

"What are they?"

"Dramamine, the non-drowsy formula."

"Why?" I asked, baffled. Even in rough waters at sea, I'd never suffered motion sickness.

"Trust me, Sam. I think you'll be glad you did."

"Why?" I asked again, shaking my head.

"Because of what I'm going to show you."

He handed me a pill. I still had half a glass of tea for washing it down, but what if it wasn't Dramamine? Was my uncle attempting to drug me? I hesitated.

"Please, Sam. Trust me."

I looked my uncle in the eye and didn't detect any malice. I shrugged, popped the pill in my mouth, and downed it with the last of my tea.

Uncle stood from his chair. "Come with me."

I followed him down a hallway and through a door to a long stairway that descended into a large, deep basement, bringing to mind a castle dungeon. Uncle led me to a large desk next to a wall where he picked up a thick manuscript and handed it to me. Its title was a formula:

$$E = Mc^2 = S(x)$$

I recognized the first part as Albert Einstein's famous formula that equated mass and energy, but his last term evaded me.

I could tell Uncle was watching my reaction. "The 'S' stands for space. The 'x' is the math I have developed over the last decade that solves the equation."

I shrugged and handed the manuscript back, having no idea what it all meant.

Frank smiled. He set the manuscript on the table and placed a hand on my shoulder. "Follow me." He led me across his cavernous basement to a huge, circular mirror that must have been ten feet in diameter. He tapped it. "Pure tungsten. It's a foot thick and it's a perfect crystal. Very happy atoms.

"Happy atoms?" I asked, raising my brow.

"Oh yes, very happy. Did you know that no metal in the universe has a higher melting point? It misses its counterpart." Uncle pointed across the room. A hundred feet away on the opposite wall was an identical ten-foot-wide mirror.

"More tungsten?" I asked.

He nodded. "Identical in every way. It misses its partner here." He tapped the tungsten mirror we stood beside. 'They were once a single crystalline entity until I carefully divorced them."

I thought it odd that Uncle was talking about slabs of metal as though they had feelings. Upon a second look, I noticed a structure the shape and size of a shoe box protruding from the center of the flat tungsten surface. "What's in the box?"

"I'll show you." He lifted the lid. Inside a white mouse looked up at us with beady little eyes and twitching whiskers. "His name is Gonzales."

I failed to stifle a laugh. Frank having a pet mouse was surprising enough, but to find one in that little box was.... Well, it was laughably weird.

"I suspect the Dramamine tablet has entered your bloodstream by now."

"Yeah, probably so," I said.

"Follow me." Uncle led me to a large gray box hanging from the wall halfway between the two tungsten mirrors and offset to one side by twenty feet.

"Watch closely. I'm going to apply an electrical charge to my two tungsten friends."

He depressed a lever and the tungsten mirror to my right developed a weird bulge. How could a foot-thick solid metal mirror do that? But it wasn't just the mirror. The whole wall of Uncle's basement seemed to bow inward. Was it an optical illusion? Uncle pressed the lever further. I heard the hum of electrical power. I looked the other way. The opposite wall was bulging inward too, its tungsten mirror leading the way.

The whole room was distorting! Was I hallucinating? What was really in that little white pill Uncle gave me? "My gosh! What's happening? Are we going to be crushed?"

"No, Sam, as living organisms of exceedingly low

entropy, we're safe."

The distortion grew worse and my stomach did flip-flops. Tongues of tungsten were approaching one another in the middle of the insanely warped room. The floor beneath me bowed up, the ceiling above sagged and the wall behind me bowed forward. It was like everything was getting pinched toward a point in the center of Frank's basement.

"Hungry tungsten," Uncle Frank said with a grin.

The tungsten tongue coming from the other side of the room had a box the same size as the one housing Gonzales. The two boxes that had been a hundred feet apart were now almost touching.

"Gonzales' loves cheddar and I know he's hungry." Uncle toggled a switch and doors in the two little boxes swung open. Gonzales leapt off the pressure plate in his box, starting a timer and landed on a pressure plate in the second box, stopping the timer.

"A hundred thirty-six milliseconds from mouse launch to mouse touchdown." Frank said, reading the digits displayed on the side of the Gonzales' new box.

He began lifting the lever, the hum decreased and the opposing walls that had nearly met in the middle of the room began to retreat and finally returned to their flat condition on opposite walls a hundred feet apart.

My stomach began to settle, but I was in a daze as I followed Uncle to the mirror on the other side of the basement. He opened the lid to the small box. Inside Gonzales was happily munching on his hunk of cheese.

"Ah, success." He looked at me with a smile. "Last time we had an unexpected electrical discharge." His smile faded. "Gonzales' cousin, Jerry, was vaporized." He sighed.

"But such are the risks of research. The thunder blew out six of my windows, making my ears ring for the next three days. I had to tweak a formula to correct the error."

He pulled a calculator from his pocket. "Let me see. 100 feet in 0.136 milliseconds. That equates to 500 mph." He looked up at me with a smile. "Speedy, huh?"

My stomach was settling but my mind was reeling. "Wha ... what did I just witness?"

"Space conversion, my boy." He smiled. "I've found a way to suck some of it up to shorten the distance between two points. By the way, the fence around my acreage is to keep people far enough away so they would never notice the visual distortion that happens when my tungsten gobbles up few hundred cubic meters of space inside my basement."

"What's all this ... uh ... space gobbling good for, Uncle?"

He eyed me with a look clearly expressing I must have had trouble finding my nose on my face. "Interstellar space travel, of course."

My eyes bulged and my mind whirled as I contemplated the implications.

"Think you can write something up?"

"Oh, yeah!" How could a scoop like this not be a shot of steroids to my journalism career?

"Good! Let's celebrate. I know a great steakhouse in town. The Internet tells me they've still got a thriving business."

* * *

When my report on Uncle Frank's space conversion hit

the news, a loud and worldwide outcry of "hoax!" arose from the physics establishment, but with a nod from Uncle, I wrote back, "Come and see."

And they did. Among the first were two tight-lipped physicists from Sedgwitz University who refused Frank's advice regarding Dramamine, but Spencer, his faithful assistant, graciously mopped up the floor afterward.

Uncle came out of his shell that night. His self-imposed isolation had come to an end. Uncle celebrated his success by taking Spencer and me out to dinner at the finest steak house in town. Over the next week or so he got reacquainted with his old friends and colleagues. Now that he had proven his technology, he explained he was immune to any barb or discouraging comment the naysayers could fling at him.

What began as a trickle became a flood. Physicists from around the world came to witness space conversion in Uncle's basement. They came as cynics and left as bug-eyed believers. Reporters and news teams stormed Uncle's mansion with their cameras and satellite dishes. Sedgwitz had found its place on the map. Accompanying a citywide economic resurgence, Uncle's reputation quickly morphed from crazy-mad-scientist to the town's finest citizen and most respected physicist. After my TV appearances with Uncle Frank, I nailed down authorship of three different Internet science columns. My career had gone stratospheric.

Two months later, Uncle called. "I've been asked to be the keynote speaker at a conference in Edinburgh sponsored by the Institute of Physics. They've hinted they'll present me with a special award. Would you like to come to Scotland with me?"

"Of course, I'll come, Uncle. When do we leave?" I knew the proceedings of the conference would provide fresh and meaty material for my science columns.

Two days later, a taxi with a chatty Pakistani driver picked Uncle and me up at an NYC hotel and delivered us to the LaGuardia airport at 5:45. a.m. We stopped at Starbucks where Uncle picked up a venti brew. Then we strolled down a mostly empty concourse and took seats at the gate C-32 where we awaited our seven-hour flight to Edinburgh.

At 6:05, half an hour before our scheduled boarding time, an amazingly attractive flight attendant in her elegantly styled red and silver outfit came through the gate doorway. From the wide-eyed, smiling faces of every man in the waiting area, I was pretty sure they all agreed with my assessment of her.

Uncle gazed at the woman with a smile, set his coffee down, and whispered to me, "I hope she's not going to inform us of a flight delay."

"Franklyn Steinberg?" she asked, focusing on Uncle.

"Yes?" His eyes lit up and he sat straight up in his chair.

"We've made special travel arrangements for you, sir."

"Really? You mean to Edinburgh?"

"To the awards ceremony, sir. Please come with me."

A lanky red-headed man seated across from us mumbled something with a distinct look of envy in his eyes.

Uncle's smile broadened. He looked at me then her. "Can my nephew come along?"

"No, sir, but the two of you won't be apart for long."

He shrugged at me with a slightly guilty look.

Tea Cozies and Terabytes: People

"Go ahead, Uncle. We've got our reservations. I'll meet you at our hotel in Edinburgh." I knew the conferees were going to honor Uncle for his discovery, but now I pictured them wining and dining him on his overseas trip with this lovely flight attendant. I could only imagine the ultra-first class accommodations he was going to enjoy on his was to Scotland.

"See you in Edinburgh, Sam," he said, glancing back before disappearing though the door and into the jet way.

I noticed he'd forgotten his coffee that remained on the little table between our chairs. I settled into my seat and wished I'd picked up something to read at the news stand. I was feeling lonely and absently gazing out the window when I saw an odd flicker above the tarmac. Did something just zip by? Nah. Probably just an odd reflection off the window.

Award Ceremony

R. D. Sadok

I felt a little guilty leaving my nephew, Sam, behind as I followed the gorgeous flight attendant down the jet way of LaGuardia's gate C-32. However, I felt sure Sam and I would reconnect at our hotel in Edinburgh later that afternoon after the Institute of Physics honored me with their luxury overseas flight. It wasn't until the next morning that the Institute planned to present me with an award for my work in space compression.

The sun was just rising when she led me to a tiny, custom aircraft parked on the tarmac, not at all the slick Gulfstream I was expecting. I stopped in my tracks and stared at the oddly-designed two-seater.

"We're flying in that?" I couldn't imagine where they'd even find room for my luggage. "This little thing is supposed to make an overseas flight?" I shook my head. "Who's going to pilot it? You?"

She stopped, turned, and melted me with her astonishingly beautiful smile. "Sir, it is a very capable transport, and I'm well-qualified to operate it."

I believed her. She drew me in like a magnet. Minutes

later, I found myself buckled into the cockpit beside her. The glass dome enclosed us provided great visibility. She pressed a button. A brief whistling sound, and a slight popping in my ears indicated the cockpit had sealed. So, it seemed this tiny craft was capable of high altitudes flight. We backed away from the gate and quickly taxied out to runway as silently as an electric golf cart.

What happened next convinced me this was all a dream and I was still asleep back in my hotel room. Without a sound, and with me barely pushed back in my seat, we zoomed down the runway like a movie in fast-forward and quickly curved upwards. The sky darkened and stars came out. I looked out to the side of the clear glass dome and saw the curvature of the earth. Moments later, the moon sailed by as speedily as passing a boulder alongside the highway.

I laughed. Yep, I've got to be dreaming. Any other possibility was too mind-boggling to consider, so I figured I might as well enjoy it. The sun was blindingly bright at first but dimmed as we exited the solar system. Soon bluish-tinted stars were sailing by like I'd seen in most episodes of Star Trek. I glanced at the lovely pilot next to me and she smiled at me. This was one sweet dream. The panoramic views both inside and outside the cockpit were breathtaking. The stars were now flying by like the snowflakes against the windshield in a snow storm. It was as though we were traveling millions of times the speed of light, patently impossible according to Einstein ... but maybe not inconceivable with space conversion.

Ah, it must have been that high-flying thought that had stimulated my marvelous dream. I wondered if she were taking me some place in particular, or if this was just going to be a joy ride around the galaxy.

Every minute or so my ears popped, but I hardly gave it a thought. Stars thinned as we rose above the galactic plane.

"My name is Ceriana," my flight attendant-turned-pilot said with that heart-melting smile of hers. "Space conversion works best in the flatter space between the galaxies."

Yep, that made sense. I smiled, now convinced my psycho-analysis of what had stimulated my dream was correct. I looked out the window and saw the Milky Way galaxy recede like the passing of a billboard on the highway. Now whole galaxies were sliding by as fast as individual stars had a minute ago.

I looked away for a moment, then looked back. Spiral galaxies abounded. Hundreds of them. Which one was the Milky Way? I'd lost track! A sudden terror seized me. I was lost in space! My dream had morphed into a nightmare.

"Wake up!" I screamed to myself. I slapped myself, then I pinched myself, but all to no avail. If not a dream, then what? A hallucination? Had someone at Starbucks spiked my coffee with something psychedelic? Where the heck was she taking me?

Ceriana took my hand. Her touch was electric and at the same time like soothing balm. My breathing steadied, and the beat of my pounding heart slowed. I looked into her eyes. In them I saw deep pools of sympathy and concern.

"You're not lost, Frank. Trust me. You are in good hands. We've come for you to honor you. Many of us to want to meet you and pay our respects."

I dared tear my gaze from her comforting eyes to look

out the window again. Nearby galaxies were flashing by too fast to be distinguished, but in the distance I could see them as tiny beads, strung together in filaments of amazing symmetry. A symmetry that could have only been formed by design, the design of the Creator. The magnitude of the universe was beyond anything I'd ever imagined and beyond what any earth-orbiting telescope had ever perceived. Even more mind-numbing was our speed of travel.

Ceriana smiled. Her eyes glistened. *Octillion L* flashed through my mind. An octillion times the speed of light. Had I thought that or...?

"Who exactly are you?" I asked, staring into her deep blue eyes.

"I'm a woman of your future, living in a culture that would never have existed without your contribution to it five hundred earth-years earlier."

I pinched myself one more time to assure myself this wasn't a dream, then I looked back at her. "You ... you mean space conversion?"

She nodded. "Yes, that and other developments that have come along since."

While I attempted to digest the implication of her words, we slowed, and I was again able to distinguish individual galaxies. Slowing more, we approached an exotic one with spirals like the Milky Way but with symmetry matching that of a complex and stunningly beautiful snow flake.

As I gazed out the window, she must have noticed my awestruck expression.

"An early shadow of what you see was Solomon's

temple."

My mind whirled, trying to comprehend. "You know of Earth's history?"

"Of course," she said, with a gentle laugh. "This galaxy, as was Solomon's temple, is an expression of honor and worship of the Creator."

As I attempted to digest what she said, we entered the galaxy. I remained speechless as we slowed through the snowstorm effect, then Starship-Enterprise-at-warp-nine, and approached a bright, golden star and an earth-like planet. Unlike earth, its coastlines were sculpted with swoops and swirls, artwork of immense creativity.

We landed in the center of what seemed to be a soccer-field-sized, heart-shaped clearing in a forest.

At the inner point of that heart was a magnificent, hundred-foot-tall tree with a multitude of large, mitten-shaped leaves cupped to receive energy from the golden sun above. Ceriana pressed a button and the transparent dome of our transport slid back. I was greeted by a fragrance reminiscent of orchids and lilies. Ceriana stepped out. I followed, feeling heavy, reminding me of a hike when I had carried a fifty-pound backpack.

"Valarnia has 1.23 g's" The thought hit me as though spoken, both the name of the planet and its gravity being 1.23 times earth's. I understood why my ears had been popping. The heavier planet held a thicker atmosphere, and the air pressure at the surface was higher. Her spacecraft had adjusted for it.

I turned and took in my surrounding and I gasped, and I shuddered. I felt my own eyes bulge.

Aliens! Monsters!

Tea Cozies and Terabytes: People

I was surrounded by a plethora of horrible, ghastly creatures, some large and some small, but all the substance of my worst nightmares. Their mingling odors clenched my stomach. Those nearest to me appeared to shrink away and darken as sweat trickled from my armpits down my sides.

Ceriana took my hand. Her touch was warm. Again, I felt that electric soothing effect. The atmosphere changed, seemed to brighten. Tension eased from my body and I breathed a sigh of relief. Sensing the vibrancy flowing from her hand, I realized Ceriana had a special gift of touch that stilled my fears and brought me peace, and clarity to my mind.

I looked around again. Forming the perimeter of the heart shaped opening were intelligent beings of awe-inspiring diversity, representing God-breathed life that had developed on a multitude of different planets. I felt a moment of guilt that quickly dissipated and was replaced with a deeper understanding of the human frailty that lead one race to display unwarranted prejudice against another. I wondered how I could communicate an apology to those around me for my fearful and judgmental thoughts.

I understand. All is forgiven and forgotten. The thought arose as a chorus from those around me who seemed to brighten and enlarge. It finally dawned on me that it wasn't necessary to generate sound waves to communicate in this gathering.

"They have come to honor you." The soundless words seemed to emanate from Ceriana large blue eyes. "They want to celebrate your God-led discovery of Space Conversion."

My name is Azwansi

Someone had wordlessly spoken. Who? I scanned the variety of beings surrounding me but didn't find the source. My attention was drawn toward the hundred-foot-tall tree at the inner point of the heart, but I didn't see any beings in that direction, only the forest behind it.

A chuckle. *It's me.*

A breeze stirred and the tree performed something between a curtsy and a bow by flexing dozens of its branches and turning its leaves to face me.

The tree was talking to me. My preconceived notion that intelligence was strictly the domain of the animal kingdom, was just blown out of the water.

"Please meet Premier Azwansi," Ceriana thought.

I swallowed. Not only had the vegetable kingdom produced an intelligent being but a leader of *273,206* planets, a number Azwansi at that moment silently communicated to me.

I looked at Azwansi with new respect and felt the warmth of his unseen smile. Only now did I see Azwansi's sparkling trunk and branches. What I first thought were glimmering reflections from the golden sun above were the flashing of uncountable of neurons. I couldn't help wondering if he was the brainiest tree in the whole universe.

Hearing a scraping sound, I turned to look. One who appeared to be a huge, reptilian version of a sea anemone approached me. It sauntered up on a dozen dark green, shimmering appendages that functioned as legs while waving twelve more similar appendages in the air, some reaching eight feet high. A third of the way from its central truck, each appendage contained an eye with slit-pupils like a cat, most of which were looking at me. Beneath each eye were mouths with almost human-looking lips that smiled at me. In one of its air-born appendages, it held a golden, wallet-sized object.

It made a chorus of soft, gurgling noises and emitted a most interesting odor while speaking to my mind, "In recognition of your critical-path achievement, that has made our intergalactic society possible, I, Zhagir, have the honor of representing our confederation by awarding you this medal."

The creature "handed" the medal to me. Embossed on it was an image of the beautiful snow flake galaxy. Beneath that swirling image was a formula in my own alphabet:

$E = Mc^2 = S(x) = T(y)$

The first two terms were Einstein's and the third was mine. The fourth was a mystery.

After I accepted the award, the formal atmosphere of the meeting ended. Everyone began to mingle and chatter. It was cacophony to my ears, but the spirit was one of country hoedown from my youth. Food of astounding variety appeared on tables, some divinely pleasant to my nose and others not so much. Depending upon their physiology, all sat down or otherwise sauntered up to the tables and enjoyed a good feast.

The next eight hours of taste-bud explosion flew by in a blur. Many approached me to congratulate me and share thoughts that included visuals of their home planets of multifaceted charm, strangeness and beauty.

Finally, the award ceremony and the after-party wound down, and we all expressed our goodbyes. Ceriana took my hand and escorted me back to her transport. As galaxies zinged by on our return trip, she responded to my unasked question about the last term of the formula embossed on my medal.

"$T(y)$ addresses time. One of Azwansi's race solved the equation.

The implications would have bowled me over if I hadn't been buckled into my seat. Energy, matter, space, and time, all parts of God's creation were somehow interchangeable, one with another.

It explained how I'd been transferred not only across the far reaches of the universe, but also five hundred years into the future. But then a question arose. Could she really take me back? Would it even be safe for her to do so? Might what I had experienced in the distant future affect my life upon returning to my own time, thereby impacting the very future I'd witnessed, possibly obliterating it? I didn't want to endanger the wonderful and amazing society I had experienced today. It was that same old paradox of what would happen to me if I went back in time and prevented my father from meeting my mother, only on a far grander scale.

Ceriana apparently picked up on my conundrum. "As described in the math of $T(y)$, many elements have to be perfectly aligned for time travel to be allowed, and in those rare cases the space-time continuum isn't disturbed." She smiled at me, that amazing smile. "Today's event with your Award Ceremony on Valarnia was one of those cases."

The galaxies slowed before a familiar spiral one came into view.

"The Milky Way?" I asked.

She nodded. We entered an arm of the galaxy. The snowstorm of stars slowed and a yellow star somewhat smaller than average came into view.

"Sol?"

She nodded. The earth showed up big, round and beautiful. We landed on the same spot of tarmac at the LaGuardia airport from which we left. After we climbed out of the transport, I glanced at my watch. I saw that eight hours had passed, but it seemed like a life-time.

"It's time to say goodbye," Ceriana said with tender sadness in her eyes as she escorted me to the jet way.

"Yes, I suppose it is." I reached out and touched her hand one last time and felt that electric vibe, the strength of her peace and joy. She turned, walked back to the tiny transport, climbed in and flitted away no more conspicuously than a sparrow taking to the air. She was gone. I sighed. I would truly miss Ceriana.

I climbed the stairs, walked down the jet way and through the door into the gate C-32 waiting area. I was amazed to see Sam standing there looking back at me.

"You're still here?" I asked. "How many hours has the flight been delayed?"

Sam looked baffled by my question. "Did you come back for your coffee?"

I followed his glance to my coffee on the table where I had been seated eight hours earlier. Others in the waiting area turned to look. They all seemed to be seated exactly where they were when I left.

"Ha!" the redheaded man seated across from Sam said. "It was all a joke, wasn't it?"

"A joke?" I asked, looking around at dozen men who had turned toward me with big grins on their faces.

"Yeah," the redhead said. "I'm talking about the cute

dish in her fancy red and silver uniform. Fat chance she was really going to escort you on some private jet all the way to Edinburgh."

A chorus of laughter broke out in the waiting area.

I had no idea how to respond, but I was getting a strange inkling. I glanced out the window and noted the sun's position was just above the eastern horizon. I walked over to the table, picked up my coffee, and took a sip. "Ow! This is still hot."

"Well, yeah, Uncle." Sam looked at me with his head cocked to one side. "What did you expect?"

"Ha!" I suddenly understood. It all had to do with that T(y) term. Ceriana had returned me to almost the moment in time we had left. Maybe a minute or two later.

A nearby load speaker blared, "Flight 2205 scheduled to depart from Gate C-32 to Edinburgh has been delayed until 7:30."

A collective groan went up from the crowd.

"Good," I said, looking Sam in the eye. "We need to talk." I led him to the far side of the waiting area where we could speak privately. "Let me tell you what happened over the last eight hours."

"Something wake you up around midnight? Sam asked.

"No. I'm talking about today."

Sam shrugged. "I'm not following you, Uncle."

"Pull out your notebook, get your pen ready, shut up, and listen."

As I began relating my amazing experience of the day, I saw a crooked smile spread across Sam's face, and I realized how far-fetched it all must sound. When I got to describing Azwansi, the telepathic tree, and Zhagir, the eight-foot-tall reptilian sea anemone, Sam cracked up, tossed his pad down on the chair, and slapped his knee.

"Uncle! Your story is a blast! When did you take up science fiction? I bet there's a magazine that would publish that, maybe an anthology somewhere. He slapped me on the shoulder and laughed again.

I shook my head, pulled my gold medal from my pocket, and hefted its weight. It proved to me that my experience was real, but who else would believe it? As far as they were concerned, the gold item in my hand could have been a trinket I picked up in a pawn shop. While pondering the $T(y)$ term embossed on the golden, snow flake galaxy, I realized my time travel had been allowed because no one on the planet would believe whatever I said about it, thus its impact on everyone who knew me would be negligible. That's why the space-time continuum was safe.

I only hoped I'd come across as properly appreciative at tomorrow's award ceremony in Edinburgh despite it being a wee bit anticlimactic.

Forever Faithful

Olive Swan

Mud clogged Andrew's mouth and nose. Rocks scraped his palms as he tried to push himself to his feet, but stronger arms pinned him to the ground. A flash of heat burned as a leather belt lashed over the back of his legs. He bit his lip, holding in the cry of pain that almost escaped, preserving his last shred of dignity.

Outside the ring of taunting boys stood Andrew's foster brother, keeping away lest he also earn the wrath of the bullies. Andrew gave him one pleading glance, but Cody flushed and slid away in self-preservation.

With a grunt, Andrew twisted, kicking his legs and knocking one of the boys off of him. The belt slashed across his knees. He jumped up and swung at the nearest boy. Mud clouded his vision and his fist whiffed past the boy, just fluttering the bully's sleeve.

"What is going on? Andrew, are you fighting?"

An adult's voice cut through the jeers.

"Andrew fell into the mud," a boy lied. "And blamed it on Justin."

Andrew had not fallen, and Justin – belt boy – had

instigated the bullying all week, undetected. Injustice burned Andrew's heart. Flicking his hands, he dislodged the excess mud. He kept his eyes lowered because he knew that if he looked at the day-camp volunteer, she would see the disgust in his hazel eyes.

"Andrew, we don't fight here. You need to conduct yourself with kindness. Remember that we are learning to build character this week."

"Yes, ma'am," he replied through pursed lips.

"It's time to come in for snack time." Her tone with the other children sounded more natural for 4th grade; not like the kindergartner tone she had used with him.

Andrew knew that his status unnerved people. Not quite family, not quite stranger, not quite anything.

In the bathroom, he splashed water on his face and his floppy bangs. The mud had begun to dry gray over his light brown hair. Back in the cafeteria for snack time, his tormentors ate Oreos and drank Sunny D, making jokes as if they hadn't just harassed him because he was a foster kid. Cody had reappeared now that the danger to him was gone; to make the betrayal even worse, he laughed along with the bullies. Cody had to attend school with these boys through high school. Why should he alienate them over a foster brother who might not even be there in fifth grade?

The next afternoon, Andrew sat cross-legged on the floor for the short lecture portion at the end of the day. A man in camouflage spoke about joining the military and the self-reliance they could learn. The group leaders handed out camo-colored paper bags to each child.

On the drive home, Andrew pulled out a silicone wristband etched with "An Army of One," a blue pen with

"NAVY" in block letters, a keychain with Air Force wings, and a notepad with an emblem. The emblem grabbed his attention. He ran his thumb over the vivid red and traced the golden eagle, globe, and anchor. He tried to sound out the words quietly, wishing he could read better.

"*An*drew."

He looked up and saw his foster mother eyeing him in the rearview mirror. "I hope you didn't get into any fights today."

"No, ma'am."

The camp counselor had informed Cody's mother about Andrew's fight, and she had not believed his defense. Why should she when his foster brother didn't back him up? Of course she would believe her own son over Andrew. That night, Andrew pulled out his notepad again. His heart calmed at the stately majesty of the eagle, the calming roundness of the design. He sounded out the words carefully out loud.

"Un-tied States Mar-eyen Cor-psuh."

He frowned and read the first word again. "Yoo-nine-ted."

That was better. United States. That's where he lived. Maybe Mar-eyen Cor-psuh was a state in the United States?

He looked back in the bag at the other military items. That meant the M-A-R-I-N-E-C-O-R-P-S was a military thing. He hid the notepad under the mattress so it wouldn't be taken from him. Whether or not Cody was a thief didn't matter. Andrew didn't trust him. Andrew didn't trust anyone.

Andrew's time with Cody's family didn't last much

longer, and the foster care system shuffled Andrew around to more homes over the next few years, his stay rarely lasting longer than a year. On his 12th birthday, he entered the van Dyke home, his black duffle bag in one hand and a plastic bag in the other with possessions he'd collected over the years. The social worker handed the van Dykes a folder of Andrew's official papers: birth certificates, social cards, and other papers regarding his status.

He stood sullenly on the square of vinyl that made up the foyer of their townhome.

"Welcome to our home, Andrew," Mr. van Dyke greeted him. He held out his hand to Andrew. Andrew handed him his duffle bag.

Mr. van Dyke chuckled. He set the bag down and picked up Andrew's hand which lay limply in his large one.

"Firm up your grip, young man," Bill encouraged kindly. "Show some confidence." Andrew's eyes widened and he looked into Mr. van Dyke's cool blue eyes; cool in color, but warm in kindness. He gave Mr. van Dyke's hand a good shake and the older man laughed. "Better. We hope you will be happy here. This is my wife, Susan. You can call me Bill."

"We'll show you where you're going to be staying. I'm sorry that our kids no longer live at home anymore so you could have siblings."

Andrew followed Susan up the stairs glancing at the photos hung stairway wall. His spirits sank. Susan and Bill's children were older. Andrew didn't think the van Dykes would be interested in adopting him. The hope for a family died a little in his heart, surprising him that he had allowed himself to have hope.

He wouldn't mind a family that didn't have children. Siblings were nice. Parents were better.

"What do you think?" Susan smiled brightly as she opened the door to a room at the top of the stairs. "My son really liked baseball, but if you want to redecorate, let us know and we'll see what we can do."

"I don't mind baseball," he replied politely.

She left him to unpack. Andrew dropped his duffle bag on the floor and began taking out the items from the plastic bag, arranging them on the desk. The clay dinosaur he'd made in a craft time at a Vacation Bible School sat in the center, protecting the other items, a little wooden box his grandmother once told him had belonged to his mom. The wooden box was the only thing he had left from both of them. Inside lay a sand dollar from a trip to the beach with the foster family he had lived with at age 6. In the center of the desk he placed his Marines Corps notepad, corners curling, colors faded, little marks and smudges earned over the last three years. It still had all its pages though.

He wanted it to last forever, so he chose not to use it.

* * *

"Ugh. I *hate* the mall."

"You wouldn't have had to come if you hadn't lied to Bill about cheating on your homework," Susan frowned. "If you want to be trusted, you have to earn our trust."

Andrew let out a disgusted grunt because he didn't have an answer.

Susan and Bill spent far too much time trying to get him to do right things. He couldn't let them know he secretly appreciated that they gave him rules and boundaries. They'd shown him innumerable mercies in the year he had been living with them. He would die before he would tell them how much he appreciated them.

Andrew dragged himself behind Susan as they entered the mall. Susan and her daughter paused at the large mall map to decide their route. Andrew glanced around at the few store fronts between the JC Penney's and Macy's anchor stores. He guessed there would be several new pairs of khaki pants in his bureau at home by the evening.

Khaki pants were forgotten when his eyes caught a familiar emblem design on the window of a storefront. He read the sign above: United States Military Recruiting Office. He glanced back at Susan. They were still deciding where to shop first, so he approached the office. A man in camo looked up from his phone when Andrew entered.

"Hello there, Son. Are you lost?"

Andrew shook his head. "I'm looking for the United States Marine Cor-psuh."

The man grinned. "This is a recruiting office for the United States Marine Corps. The best fighting force in the whole world. A brotherhood in arms."

Andrew's eyes lit up.

"How did you become brothers?"

"Through training and traditions and hardship. We're a brotherhood of fighters."

To Andrew's delight, the recruiter next explained the symbolism of the emblem that Andrew had long admired and translated the motto. "*Semper Fidelis* means 'Always Faithful.'"

That settled it. "What do I have to do to join?"

"Finish your high school education first. Stay fit. Take care of yourself. When you join, they'll whip you into shape, make you a warrior."

Andrew's mind flew back to the park district day camp and being thrown into the mud. Years later, the humiliation still rankled. "I want to be a warrior." *So the bullies can't beat me up again.*

"That's a start."

Andrew eyed him warily. "Will they still take me if I cheated on a test?

The man covered his mouth quickly to hide a smile and then gave Andrew a somber, appropriately adult look. "Our motto is duty, honor, and country. We conduct ourselves in a noble way. Do you know what that means?"

"I think it means that I shouldn't cheat or tell lies or steal."

"That's right."

"Okay, I won't! And when I graduate, I'll come back here and sign up for the Marine Corps."

"I look forward to it," and the recruiter saluted at him.

Puffing out his chest, Andrew saluted him back and then ran out to find Susan.

* * *

Andrew lived at the van Dyke's house until he was 16 and they were the happiest four years of his life. He hoped that it would never have to leave. After Christmas, three and a half years into his stay, he noticed that Bill and Susan had whispered conversations and shared worried looks; once they ended their conversation guiltily when he entered the room.

After New Year's they called him into the den.

"We have some bad news," Bill said. Susan wiped her eyes with a crumpled tissue.

Andrew already knew. He braced himself.

"My company is moving me out of state."

The death knell.

"We've looked into retiring or getting a job with another company, but in this economy —."

"No," Andrew stopped them. "It's fine. I get it. We all knew it was going to be temporary. I was at least hoping I could stay until I was 18, but I'll be fine. I've got the Marines to look forward to."

Susan pulled him into a hug. He could feel her tears on his hair. Andrew wished he could say it was okay, but it wasn't. He had hoped for more time with the van Dykes, but he couldn't be taken out of state. They couldn't stay. By the time an adoption went through, he would probably be 18.

You're a survivor; you don't need them anyway.

"Really, I'll be okay."

"My boss said we don't have to move to South Carolina until the school year is over. And we want you to know that if you want to move near us when you're out of school, you will be welcome."

How would Andrew get from Ohio to South Carolina?

"I'm still planning on entering the military. Maybe I'll come see you on my leave."

"And when you get out, take advantage of the GI Bill and go to college," Bill encouraged him. "We'll be praying that nothing keeps you from the military."

Andrew had not considered this fearful possibility and his sorrow at leaving the van Dykes now became dread for his future. He tossed and turned that night until falling into a fitful sleep where he was thrown from the recruiting office and had to walk past all his old foster families hearing their jeers. He woke with sweat beading on his forehead moments before his alarm blared in his ear. He lay for a few minutes staring up at the ceiling.

My own family didn't want me. What if the military won't take me either?

Would he find his place anywhere?

The van Dykes and social worker dropped Andrew off at the new foster house. As Andrew hoisted his suitcase over his arm, Bill held out his hand to him.

"I wish you luck, Andrew, and we'll be in touch. Take this gift and think of us when you use it."

Andrew took the wrapped gift and grasped Bill's hand firmly, thankful for all he had learned from this man. The bitterness had dissipated, only to be replaced by grief that he didn't have more time with them. The social worker smiled encouragingly at him, but he didn't return the smile.

He faced the front door as he emotionally prepared for a new home. The awkward introductions and forced small talk. Spending the first few days feeling out the personalities in the house and sizing up the other children to decide if they would be allies or enemies. He shouldered his bag and forced a pleasant look on his face as the social worker rang the doorbell.

Another home. Another family.

Tea Cozies and Terabytes: People

In the bedroom that he would be sharing his foster brother, Andrew unwrapped the present from Bill. His breath caught. In the center of the black leather portfolio, about the size of a paperback book, was a medal medallion, embossed with the eagle, globe and anchor and the words around the outside "United States Marine Corps." Clutching it to his chest, Andrew held on as if he were giving Bill and Susan one last hug.

They thought he *could* make it. For them, he would.

* * *

Marine Corps Basic Training

Mud filled Andrew's mouth and the dust clogged his throat. Every muscle ached, even muscles that they had forgotten to inform him about in high school anatomy. His palms were scraped. He was pretty sure he had oozing blisters on his feet. But the men around him were not bullies, but his brothers, following him through the night course during the last event of The Crucible, the most physically, mentally, and emotionally grueling time in his life.

Hold on. Make it through one more day. The mantra repeated itself in his head until morning.

The last day started with a nine-mile hike with full pack on his back. Each step felt like he was walking on bricks that were stabbing nails into his feet. Despite the soreness, his heart soared as the Parris Island Iwo Jima Memorial greeted the recruits at the end of their journey. He dropped his pack and joined the other recruits in rows facing the Memorial. He didn't hear much of the drill instructor's congratulatory message, focusing instead on his goal achieved. He'd done it!

The drill instructor reached Andrew and placed into his left palm a black-painted brass emblem.

Andrew's thumb traced over the ridges and points of the eagle, globe and anchor. The Sergeant, who'd made his life a living hell for the last three months, smiled at him and held out his hand.

"Welcome to the Corps, Marine. Well done."

Marine. No longer a recruit, but a Marine. And Andrew shook his hand, firmly and confidently, body aching, heart light.

He had found his home and his brothers.

Forever Family

Olive Swan

The young woman approached the door at a quick, mincing walk familiar to those of cold climates and icy paths. One hand gripped the handle of a guitar case, the other held her scarf to her nose. Andrew hurried to intercept her, crunching over the salt on the sidewalk as he jogged up to the door. Their eyes met as he held the door for her. Between the knit beanie pulled low over her forehead and above the flannel scarf, two dark blue eyes twinkled with merriment. She released the scarf and smiled at him in thanks as she let him carry the guitar case.

"Here for the student outreach tonight?"

He nodded. "I'm a volunteer."

She led him to the small anteroom on the other side of the student commons. They passed helpers setting up chairs and a sound system.

She unwound her scarf, the ends of her blonde ponytail lay on her shoulder and the ends curled against her neck. "We're always glad to have new volunteers." She stuck out a mittened hand. "I'm Marissa Benson."

"Andrew McCleod."

"I have to keep my fingers nimble for playing," she explained as she pulled off the mittens and noticed him looking at the thin pair of gloves she wore underneath.

Later, he watched enraptured as her long, slender fingers danced along the fretboard as she led the 100+ college students in singing. Everything about her seemed so lyrically feminine, even her name. *Marissa*. He had been tasked to help with the sound board, but spent more time watching the vivacious blonde at the front. He had been undecided about committing to volunteer at the Thursday night outreach. Now he wished he had volunteered several semesters ago.

The 1:00 pm Design Fundamentals 101 class was a foundational class for Freshmen graphic design majors, requiring one of the largest classrooms on campus. Marissa felt out of place as a senior amongst the sea of freshmen and sophomores. She did a double take at seeing a familiar face when she surveyed the room for a good seat. Andrew looked up as she noticed him. A shy smile came to his face and he motioned to the desk next to him. She made her way through the rows and slid into the chair next to his.

"I wasn't expecting to see you before the next outreach."

"A happy coincidence, I hope," he replied.

She flushed and nodded. "Are you going to come back next week?"

"Yes, I decided to commit for the rest of the semester."

She appreciated the solemnity in his vow. "Decided to commit." As if he had made a contract with himself.

"Would you like to meet at the café for a hot drink before outreach next Thursday? Surely that will help keep your fingers warm and nimble."

She chuckled. "I'd like that, thanks."

His smile lifted into a wide grin. "Great! We can set up the details after next Wednesday's class."

"I think that's a plan," she whispered as the professor approached the lectern to start the class.

Common Grounds Café

"Have you chosen a partner for the graphic design team project?" Andrew asked Marissa.

She put down her drink; this week's choice had been hot tea. She chose a different drink every time they met at the café. "I haven't. Wanna pair up?"

You have no idea how much.

"Absolutely. I've been trying to think what we could make a poster of?"

"Hmm, we could make a poster for my senior recital, or the senior class party or the...oh, wait, why not Thursday outreach?"

"A perfect idea!"

"We make a perfect team." She gave him a high-five. "So, what made you choose the design class for your art elective?"

"I'm basically the in-house IT and web guy at StreamBig, a small web design and development company. I'll go full-time when I graduate, and they may need me to help them design some of their small projects. Why are you taking the class?"

"To help me with marketing my business. Once I get my degree in music education, I want to teach privately. That means creating a website, business cards, posters, flyers, you name it! I thought I should get some design principles under my belt since I'll probably be creating those things myself."

"Well, if I can see about getting you a discount at StreamBig for your website, let me know."

"You don't have to do that."

"If I can help, I want to. What kind of music are you going to teach?"

"Piano, guitar, maybe do vocal instruction. I taught my younger siblings how to read music and play piano."

"How many siblings do you have?"

"Six."

"Six!"

"Yep. Nolan, Olivia, Patrick, Quentin, Rachelle and Sabrina. My parents like big families … and the alphabet." She grinned.

"I guess your house was chaotic growing up."

"Could I tell you stories! I wish we had time, but we should probably head over to the meeting room and get set up for Outreach."

This is it. All or nothing.

"Maybe we could… go to dinner sometime so we could have more time to talk?"

She searched his face, a shy look crossing her own. "Are you asking me out?"

"I am."

"Oh good, I was hoping you were."

He let out his breath and his grin stretched across his

face.

* * *

Aside from being musically gifted, or perhaps because of it, Marissa had the timing and facial expressions of a story-teller and the accounts of her childhood had Andrew laughing all through their dinner.

"You sound very close." Andrew hoped he didn't sound envious.

"My sisters and I will probably be best friends when we're all older, and my brothers are great too when they're not getting on my nerves. You know how brothers are, living to tease."

He gave her a tight smile. He did not know. His birth sister had been adopted by a family soon after their mother abandoned them.

Foster siblings often acted differently with him. Even if he got along with them, he always sensed a wall between them and him. The light in Marissa's face when she talked about her family worried him. What would she say if she found out that he didn't have a family?

"I don't mean to monopolize the conversation," she said. "I've been talking about myself too long."

"I like learning about you. My life is just about work and school. Once I graduate, it'll just be about work. Thankfully I like my job."

"Did you have to take a few years to work before starting college?"

"I spent four years in the Marine Corps."

"I wondered why you seem older than the other

students."

"And why I display such obvious maturity," he said with mocking arrogance.

She laughed. "Clearly."

He loved the sound of her laughter. He could spend his lifetime listening to it.

* * *

"Don't look so glum, my parents will love you," Marissa assured Andrew as they made their way up to the Benson house.

Andrew relaxed his fist and smiled down at her. "Okay, I'll try to be on my best behavior."

The door was flung open and a teen boy announced to the neighborhood. "You're here!"

"Hi, Quentin." Marissa gave him a big smooch which he wiped away with a look of distaste.

Inside, the rest of the family gathered around for introductions. Diane and Kenneth Benson pushed through their children to greet Andrew with warm smiles. Marissa linked her arm through Andrew's. "Mom and Dad, I want you to meet Andrew McCleod."

"We've heard so much good about you, Andrew. We're glad you're able to come to dinner tonight."

They took a seat on the couch. Sabrina squeezed between Marissa and the couch's arm and put her skinny arm around Marissa's neck, resting her head on Marissa's shoulder. The other family members circled around on the floor, Diane and Kenneth in their recliners.

Marissa could feel Andrew's tension as the family

started peppering him with questions. Gradually, she noticed him relax as he got used to the chaos. He didn't get a chance to answer all the questions, since he was too polite and wanted to know about their lives too. Did he really *have* to know how Olivia's community college classes were going?

"Marissa says you were in the Marines," Nolan asked. "What was that like?"

"Easily the best and worst experience of my life." Andrew laughed.

This invited more questions, and they talked about his military service for several minutes.

"Kenneth, I've heard that you like to fish."

The kids groaned as Kenneth's face lit up at Andrew's question. Marissa's father was a man dedicated to integrity and honesty in everything except his outlandish fish stories. Marissa threw her mother a pleading glance.

Diane put her hand on Kenneth's arm. "Sweetheart, dinner is ready, so why don't we get seated and then you can continue your conversation."

"Or not," Marissa mumbled under her breath.

Patrick and Quentin, teenagers either joined at the hip or at each other's throats depending on the minute, now shoved each other out of the way to be the one to sit on the other side of Andrew at the dinner table, Andrew foiled their plans when he took a seat by Diane, pulling out the chair for her after seeing that Marissa was seated.

Dinner proceeded smoothly, even Rachelle began to engage in the conversation. Soon, she was laughing along as Andrew found her a good-natured participant to his teasing. Marissa was impressed how quickly he had figured out her siblings. At 11, Rachelle was trying to assert her older childhood status rather than being seen as just a playmate to 8-year-old, Sabrina. Most people who didn't know her well overlooked her sharp sense of humor. Marissa gave thanks that her family all seemed to enjoy having Andrew over.

"Thank you so much for this evening," he said to them all as he put on his coat.

"I'll walk you out to the car," Marissa offered.

"How are you getting to school tomorrow?" he asked.

"Mom will drop me off after we go shopping for my recital dress."

"I hope you have fun," he said as they stood by his car, shivering slightly in the chilly air.

"We will. Mom and I get along really well."

He kicked at a stone. "I'm glad of that, I can tell why you and your family are close. I had a fun night tonight and enjoyed meeting them."

"They enjoyed meeting you," she assured him.

He seemed tense and she put her hands on his arms to reassure him. "Trust me, they like you…. I like you."

"I like you too."

They paused just a beat, the air sizzling between them and then leaned in, their lips meeting in a sweet kiss. The kiss lasted a few beautiful moments before a young voice yelled from the porch. "EWWW, Mommy! They're kissing. Gross!"

Marissa whirled around red-faced. "Sabrina!"

She ran toward the house as Sabrina let out a shriek and rushed inside as Andrew's laughter rang out in the night behind them.

* * *

Tea Cozies and Terabytes: People

Marissa stretched her fingers preparing for her practice. The cold, silent practice room in the music building had become a familiar friend over the last four years. She liked this specific room best. The piano was the same brand as the one her parents owned since her childhood. Even when she used to bang on the keys at age 3, she had known she had wanted to play. Her parents started her in lessons at age 5 and she had never stopped. Maybe she enjoyed the feeling of bringing music out of silence. Or perhaps surrounding herself in music hid her sibling-created pandemonium.

She ran through her scales and arpeggios, the familiar movements allowing her mind to wander to a piano bench far in the past, hers and Olivia's legs swinging as Marissa helped her younger sister learn the scale of C Major. For too many months Marissa wrapped herself in music to perfect the execution of a piece. Sometimes she forgot to enjoy the music. That's what she had wanted when she decided to be a teacher, to help others find that same joy in music that she had.

Pausing to lay out the pages of a recital piece, her eyes glazed over as she looked into the future and another little girl sat next to her on the piano bench as she helped her with her scales. Not a sister but a daughter. The image changed to a son.

Marissa had pictured herself with children before, but now the dream seemed within reach. She really liked Andrew, maybe even loved him. Did he love her? Was he interested in marriage and family? She played a C minor arpeggio. She knew nothing of Andrew's family, and wondered if his reticence stemmed from trouble with parents. Would coming from a bad childhood keep him from wanting his own family? If he didn't want children, did they have a future?

Shaking her head, she forced her mind back to the music on the stand. She had a recital piece to master. Once she got her diploma in her hand, she could worry about getting a ring on her finger.

* * *

"Are your parents coming to graduation?"

Andrew stiffened at Marissa's question as they sauntered from the café to the meeting room for their last Thursday outreach.

"Sadly, no. Do you want my tickets?"

"I was hoping to meet them."

He searched for words. "I'm… sorry that I don't have a close family like you do, Marissa."

"It's okay, I'm just sad for you. I mean, if you don't have family, what do you have?"

Shame settled over his shoulders. He had known too much rejection in his young life. Too many families that hadn't wanted him. Would Marissa wonder what was wrong with him because he had never been adopted? What if the Bensons decided they didn't want him either?

He fought an intense desire to pull away. Why continue with a relationship where there was bound to be hurt? For he knew that there would be. Maybe not his, but Marissa's when she found out she was dating a man without his family and without a desire to find them.

"I know family is important to you," he mumbled.

She nodded. "Very."

A weight settled on his shoulders as he realized what he had to do.

* * *

Andrew typed "McCleod" into the search bar and hovered over the ENTER key. Did he *really* want to do this?

His stomach churned as he considered what he knew of his mother. Neither of her kids' fathers stuck around. She cared more about drugs and alcohol than she did her children and had not fought for custody when they were taken from her. He had lived with a grandmother who had died before he was six. His mother never returned, and he didn't even know his father's last name. McCleod was his mother's name.

He had lived a quarter century without wanting to know about them, but now he was dating Marissa with intentions to propose. How could he give her the world when he couldn't even give her his family?

He took a deep breath and punched the button. The research website he had chosen returned with an answer in milliseconds.

"No results found."

Relief washed over him and he exited the website. There were other websites to search, but every time he would type the URL into the browser, his spirits would sink. He sat back in his chair, the glow of the lamp in the corner of his work desk the only light in the office. He signed off the computer. Taking several breaths, he considered his options. Finding his mother? Not smart. Finding his father? Impossible. Finding his sister? Unwise. He had no desire to pop into her life and upset her. Andrew reached into his desk and found his Marine Corps notepad, dropped mechanically into a paper bag by a park district volunteer, but carefully preserved for two decades. The cardboard backing was bent, but the notepad was still unused except for a small mark near the corner when he once tested an ink pen.

He ran his finger over the paper thinking how often he wanted to use it but had been afraid to use it up. He snorted.

Ridiculous.

This paper was meant to be used. So the notepad wouldn't last forever. How much did they cost to buy online?

He picked up a pen and hovered over the paper for just a moment more until he forced himself to write. And he wrote. By the time he left work at midnight, only a few blank pages remained.

* * *

After graduation, Andrew and Marissa's lives diverged as Andrew moved into an apartment near his job and Marissa returned home to teach and save money. Their relationship stayed strong though it now took place over phone calls and texts more than seeing each other daily at college.

Their conversations gradually shifted toward the future and their life goals. Andrew liked this. He wanted to look forward to where they could go together and see what dreams they had in common, rather than look to the past.

For their seven-month anniversary, they planned a fancy dinner in the city. Andrew checked his suit in the mirror, nodded in approval and then added the last piece — a ring box in his pocket. Tonight was the night. He was going to propose to Marissa. In the other pocket of his suit coat, he had the folded pieces of notepad paper upon which he had drafted a proposal months ago.

"I thought my life would get less hectic after college, but I'm as busy as ever," Marissa said as they drove downtown. "I'm teaching more students every month, but I still can't support myself and get my own place. And forcing my siblings to be silent for good portions of the day is well-nigh impossible."

"What about the music school where you interviewed?"

"It would be more lucrative to teach there, but knowing the area where it's located, it would be teaching kids whose parents are making them taking lessons for social status. I'd rather teach for free to people who want to learn than take pay from people who just want to impress their snooty friends." She sighed.

Andrew squeezed her hand. Lord willing, she would never need to teach as her main income. They might not have much on his salary, but he would bend over backwards to support her. He had lived with families of different economic statuses and the amount of money the family had didn't have any bearing on whether they were greedy or generous. It wasn't about what was in the bank account but in one's heart.

He wanted to give Marissa a home and family filled with love. He hoped she wanted the same thing. With him.

* * *

"I'm trying to decide between the cheesecake and the tiramisu. What do you think?" Marissa looked up to see Andrew gazing at the city lights. Tension lined his face. He turned back to her and his face relaxed.

"Did you decide on dessert?"

"I'll go with cheesecake."

"Good choice."

"You've been quiet, tonight, Andrew." Fear played at the back of her mind. Was he planning to dump her? "Is everything okay?"

"I'm sorry, I've been thinking."

"About us?"

He nodded. "When I was a little boy, I got a Marine Corps notepad. I'd never been so drawn to something as that logo. In a world of betrayal and upheaval, it seemed so solid and trustworthy. I decided to join the Marines and I never regretted it. Even when it was difficult, it gave me purpose. Sometimes you just know what it is you want, as if your heart has found a home."

She nodded, even as a delicious tingle began to crawl up her spine. Her hands became clammy.

He pulled out a black velvet box from his pocket and she inhaled sharply, her vision blurring for a second. He took her hand. "Marissa," his voice came out soft and warm, matching his hazel eyes. "Marissa, when I met you it didn't take me long to realize that I knew what I wanted. I wanted you as my wife.

He came over and knelt down on one knee. Her heart thumped in her chest and her hand shook in his; tears brimmed over.

"Will you marry me?"

"Yes!" she blurted out, relief releasing her heart from fear.

She heard applause around them as he kissed her. Somehow the ring ended up on her finger and someone was taking a photo, but it was all a blur. The next thing she knew, she was floating out of the restaurant with their cheesecakes in to-go bags. She was engaged!

It wasn't until they were halfway home that she interrupted their planning to ask.

"Did we even pay the bill?"

* * *

Andrew opened the Benson's door after a brief knock. Diane insisted things were too busy to keep answering the door for him and invited him to come on in. The women sat hunched over invitations, envelopes, and RSVPs slips strewn across the dining room table.

"Let's get some of this cleaned up before supper," Diane ordered her daughters. "Last thing we want is food stains on the invitations."

"Have you finished picking out the music for your wedding?" Kenneth asked over dinner.

Marissa shook her head, her mouth full of green beans.

"Marissa warned me that the music would take the longest time," Andrew admitted. "Something about her having high standards or something?"

He threw her a cheeky grin.

Diane looked up from the papers she had by her left elbow. "Andrew, where is the rest of your list for invitations? Did you email it to me? We just have a William and Susan van Dyke in South Carolina, but no other names or addresses for your family members."

A heavy silence hung in the air.

"Does your family even know about me?" Marissa asked suddenly.

Andrew froze. He should have known that this question would come. After successfully dodging it for months, he had come to believe he wouldn't have to answer. He stared at his plate. The children had all become unusually silent; he sensed their eyes on him as the silence stretched. He stiffened his spine. It had been a lovely dream, but now it was time to wake up.

"I don't have a family."

He flung the words out like a gauntlet, daring someone to pick them up and challenge him. He still couldn't look anyone in the eyes.

"Why didn't you tell me?"

He finally turned to Marissa. He had deluded himself to think that they could build a life without her knowing this. Not only was he an outcast, but he hadn't even been able to bring himself to tell her. How could he explain the specter of rejection that hovered over his life? An unadoptable — and therefore unlovable — child.

"You don't have a family?" Quentin repeated, face furrowed, unable to conceive of such a thing. Andrew hoped he never had to.

"No. I don't have a family. I've been in foster homes since I was younger than Sabrina." He shrugged. "I joined the Marines because I knew that without somewhere to go, I'd end up on the streets or ... dead." He knew the stats and how incredibly blessed he was that he was educated and employed. "The odds have been against me from the start."

His shoulders slumped and he returned his gaze to his plate.

"Who you gonna tell?" his childhood bullies had taunted him before shoving him into mud puddles and lockers. "You gonna call your dad? Oh right. You don't have one."

Without a family, you don't belong. He had heard the message loud and clear. Something is wrong with you. You're broken.

Soft arms reached around his neck and Marissa's face rested on his shoulder. He looked up in surprise. Rachelle, unusually moved, pushed her chair out and came around the table and threw her arms around him. He choked up as the rest of the siblings surrounded him, wrapping them in their arms and their love.

With a voice filled with love, tears, and humor, Marissa whispered, "You have a family now."

* * *

Andrew stood in the lobby of the church as the wedding guests streamed out of the reception hall to gather outside to throw the rice on the newly-weds.

"It was a beautiful wedding," Susan van Dyke said as she hugged Andrew. "Thank you for inviting us."

"Thank you for coming and sitting in for my parents."

Bill rested his hand on Andrew's shoulder. "We were honored."

Diane herded her kids past Andrew. "Marissa's coming," she informed him, and followed Bill and Susan outside where Kenneth guided the long black limo to the end of the line of well-wishers.

Andrew was left alone in the lobby. He looked down at his left hand and ran his thumb over the cool, solid gold band. How unfamiliar the ring felt on his finger, yet how appropriate. He had found his place, his purpose.

His wife joined him wearing a smile that would captivate him the rest of his life.

"Ready to go?" she asked.

He clasped her hands in his. "More than. Let's go start our forever."

The Age of Silicon

Antoinette Yvette Mousseau

"James, if I lose my job because I fixed this problem, could you finish copying my course work files when they walk me out? I made the mistake of putting a lot of them on my work computer." Cindy made the request simply and without feeling.

"Sure thing, but you shouldn't get fired just because you were the only one who could fix our code," James replied.

"One would hope, but 'should' and 'is' are not always in alignment," Cindy replied.

She gathered up her personal belongings into her backpack. They were few but special: a partially filled sketch book that she rarely opened but always kept on hand, a broken calligraphy pen that idled in the spine of the sketch book, and a couple books on C++ coding. "Remember, James, you always have to do your own garbage clean up in C++ to avoid memory leaks and keep the code from crashing. Java will do it for you periodically, but C++ will allow you to create memory leaks. You have to be very careful about allocating memory, and freeing up the memory that is no longer in use. Humans are the same way – you need to actively break the links to memories that no longer serve, or else the human will crash, too – but I digress."

Laughter from around the corner broke their conversation, as Zach exited the director's office with a smug smile and a swagger. James and Cindy didn't look up. They had spent the last week fixing Zach's code. Zach stopped in front of Cindy's tidy desk. "Don would like to speak with you," he said, and moved on.

A few moments later, Cindy was alone on the bleak cold street of Roosevelt Road, unemployed. Her team had just barely missed an important client's deadline for a new software application. Cindy's responsibility was to debug the code before release. Since debugging took longer than expected, she was blamed for the missed deadline and was asked to leave. It didn't matter that the troublesome code always came from Zach, who spent more time schmoozing with their boss than thinking through the code.

"Spare change?" The corner mendicant could not tell that she was crying, courtesy of the cold soft rain and rippling wind. Cindy handed him her empty change purse and said, "I have nothing more to give." Cindy kept telling herself that it didn't matter what happened. Today was her last day anyway.

Eventually, she climbed the twenty-five floors to reach the three-bedroom apartment that she shared with five roommates whom she rarely saw. She had told them that she was collecting apple seeds for replanting part of an orchard back home that had been lost to fungus attack. Fifty apple seeds were the estimated lethal dose for an average human. Cindy had collected nearly five hundred of them, from various apples throughout the preceding fall semester. The seeds needed to be crushed to release the active ingredient, amygdalin. One of her roommates owned a coffee grinder, which would have made the task quick, but Cindy ground the apple seeds by hand with a mortar and pestle, in five separate batches.

She picked up the bowl of crushed apple seeds, drew a spoonful toward her lips … and decided she should write some last words to the world. She put down the bowl and took up her beloved pen and sketchbook. Words rarely came to her, but images poured in, so Cindy decided on a self-portrait rather than a suicide note.

There were two Cindys. The first was made of long lines of impeccable white marble, chiseled into life with air and light. Cindy the White moved with a flourish and was always doing. As soon as she sprang from the sketchbook, she began scribbling away into her own sketchbook. Cindy the White had eyes with depth and vision, but no other facial features, no mouth, and no cheeks to smile with.

The second Cindy was small, infantile, and scrunched like a gargoyle. Cindy the Small had chubby hands, poor vision, and a menacing perpetual scowl, like that of a demon slave who had long lost faith in tears. Cindy the Small rolled out of the sketchbook and into a dark corner to sulk.

The sketches complete, Cindy returned to the bowl of amygdalin. "Is this how it all ends?" she asked the other Cindys. The small one growled, "Finish it unless you are a coward. Finish this futile life. You have nothing left to give." The white one asked whether there were any more beautiful sketches for her to draw, and whether she would like to watch herself draw them. Cindy scooped the crushed apple seeds into a plastic sandwich bag and labeled it, "Activated Carbon, do not eat." Cindy the White threw the bag into the trash. Cindy the Small fished it back out of the trash, along with a banana peel, candy wrapper, and other undesirables. The mass of gargoyle, seeds, and trash rolled into another dark corner.

A feisty knock at the door brought logical reasoning back to Cindy. She hadn't planned on being there anymore and was now thirty minutes late for her date. Brandon stumbled in with a dozen blood red roses that drooped for lack of water. Cindy prepared a fresh vase for the thirsty roses. "Do you still want dinner?" Brandon asked, more than a little irritated.

"I'm so sorry for making you wait," Cindy apologized and hugged him.

"I know how you can make it up," Brandon replied, drawing her into his arms. Cindy resisted. "We've been dating for three months," he continued, exasperated. "You said you'd be ready by now."

"I did not say so," Cindy protested, appalled at such poor form. Brandon was dark haired, smooth, and had arms the size of Cindy's waist. He was a powerful ally, and a powerful foe.

"I thought all of you spiritual humanist hippies were supposed to be easy," he said, "None of this 'my body is a temple' sort of thing."

Cindy the Small rolled around at Brandon's feet, cooing and cawing, but the real Cindy chose the response of

Cindy the White. She looked at Brandon with the expressionless intransigence of white stone and ordered, "Get out of my apartment."

"It was a joke," he pleaded.

"Get out of my apartment," Cindy repeated. Brandon reminded her of her brother for the last time. He left. The roses turned white and stayed behind. They were no longer of any use to him.

As his footsteps faded away, Cindy remembered that it was her birthday, today. Brandon had brought her flowers for her birthday, and she was going to have to celebrate alone. She wondered if there was at least another bit of chocolate candy in the cupboard, in lieu of friendship and cake. The front door opened again, and blood drained from Cindy's face, as she feared that Brandon had returned.

"Happy Birthday, Princess!" It was her father! "I brought you some cake. Oh, and this guy said he had some kind of thumb drive for you. He was waiting downstairs." James appeared from behind. "Was that Brandon who just left?" Her father looked at her sternly. "He won't be coming back anymore."

"What happened?" Cindy asked.

"He might come back," James explained, "but your dad whacked him with a ladder while pretending to be the maintenance guy."

"You helped." Dad smiled.

"This kid was standing in front of the elevator, punching in wrong numbers to the telecomm, cursing, calling the wrong people. He ate your chocolate waiting to piggyback someone. Finally he found someone to follow up. He left the chocolate down here so he could pick it up on the way out." Dad continued, "So I see the light is out by the elevators. I run into James, and he helps me find a ladder and some spare light bulbs."

Cindy laughed. "That is such a Dad thing to do."

"I wanted my little princess to be safe," he explained. "James helped me change the light bulb. I was cleaning up when the punk came back down. He went to the end table to pick up the chocolate, and I picked up the ladder, turned around, and whacked him in the back."

When the laughter subsided, Cindy asked James, "You brought my thumb drive?"

"Mostly," James said. "I didn't have much time, and there were a lot of files. I was able to transfer all the recent ones, from this last semester, onto a thumb drive. I had to stop copying when the HR lady showed up."

Cindy exhaled with relief. "Perfect. We all need a little bit of garbage clean up in our lives."

Not to be outdone, Dad chimed in, "I got a present for my little girl." He presented a new sketchbook and calligraphy pen. "I thought you could use a new set, and some nice blank paper."

"Wonderful!" exclaimed Cindy. "Tomorrow starts a new blank page."

The old sketchbook and the old Cindys were archived into the waste basket. Cindy felt a small pang of regret at losing Cindy the White, but knew that the next sketch would be even better.

Age of Iron

Antoinette Yvette Mousseau

Why did I do that? Cindy thought, as she watched blood dribble from her hand from a wound that she inflicted upon herself. She immediately thought of her eleventh birthday, the only childhood birthday that she remembered. In retrospect, it should have been a perfect day with balloons, cake, and smiling friends. Instead, Cindy wished that it were as inconsequential and forgettable as all the other birthdays and all the other days.

* * *

The first hint of morning was the sound of keys jingling like bells, and the slow, heavy footsteps of Cindy's father entering the kitchen and trying not to wake anyone up. Daddy was back from work. A clatter of dog nails frantically greeted Daddy. Cindy grabbed her blanket and ambled out of bed to give Daddy a hug.

"Go to bed, Princess. Look how filthy I am," he said as he scooped her up into his great arms, each of which was half as thick as Cindy's entire torso. "Happy Birthday. Are you eleven now?" Princess nodded. "Here, I got you something. Sorry I didn't wrap it." He crinkled away a plastic bag to reveal a drawing pad and calligraphy set. Cindy's eyes lit up with delight and she and her father embraced until the dog insisted on his own participation in the hug. "Ok, go back to bed now. You have school today."

"It's Saturday," said Cindy.

"You still have to go to bed. Me too. I'm tired."

Cindy scampered back to her bedroom with her new drawing pad and calligraphy pen.

"I'm eleven!" thought Cindy Amelia Connor. She considered going back to bed, but instead opened the window into the brisk dark air, saying, "Good morning, Greenville! I'm eleven." She tip-toed across the bone cold morning tiles to the bathroom scale and waited while the dial bounced and settled. Seventy-eight pounds. She smiled and looked forward to eating a whole piece of chocolate birthday cake.

Cindy slid back to her bedroom and slipped on her bright pink princess dress. She picked up her calligraphy pen, and transformed it into an ebony wand. She spun three times and became Princess Cinderella, the demi-goddess. The bare white bedroom walls became the grey interior of stone castle blocks in a high tower. Her vizier entered and bowed, "Your majesty. You have many visitors today, no doubt to wish you good health and fortune on your birthday."

"Thank you, Rasputin," replied the Princess. "Let us see our first guest." She twirled her wand and her stack of books on the floor turned into a gilded chair engraved with roses. Rasputin stood at her right as she sat down.

Tea Cozies and Terabytes: People

A tall man entered. "Dear Cinderella, may the gods bless you on your birthday. I was sent by your father to inform you of your new powers as demi-goddess of the skies. You now have the ability to make birds. Your father bids that you practice, and that you use your powers for good, not evil." He warned, "Without skillful practice, your ability may be turned against you. Here is a gift from Zeus." The messenger presented her with a beautifully bound notebook full of unlined blank pages. The notebook had gilded paper edges, a pink leather cover, and a single delicate pansy adorning the front. The Princess could hardly contain a smile as she imagined all the wonderful drawings with which she would fill up the book.

A scruffy man with a long beard entered next. "Your majesty," he bowed deeply, "There is an outbreak of Lyme disease across the Enchanted Lake of your kingdom. Eighty people died of the disease last week, and they are in great distress."

"Sir, have you forgotten what day it is?" asked the vizier.

The man looked about himself in confusion. "Ah, of course," he stammered, "Great blessings, good fortune, love, health, and all the best of fate on the occasion of your birthday, dear Princess. The people of East Greenville have all lit a candle on your birthday to remember your greatness, your goodness, and your generosity."

Princess Cinderella listened with patience and gratitude, and waved away the compliments with her wand, saying, "Thank you, sir, for alerting me to the distress of my people. You will return to East Greenville with twenty Guinea Fowl, and release them to eat the ticks carrying

Lyme disease. Please wait patiently." The Princess waved her wand and her drawing table swept into place in front of her. She sketched a bird, waved her wand, and the bird rose from the pages as a beautiful guinea fowl, without feathers because she forgot to draw them in.

"How wondrous!" cried the visitor. The Princess sketched alive more guinea fowl, this time with feathers, and the good sir left with twenty of them following his path.

"Rasputin, I will have no more visitors. Instead, I will practice creating sky creatures," said the Princess with her airy voice.

"Ah, wise choice, enlightened one," replied Rasputin. "I will ask that the remaining appointments be rescheduled." He bowed and left.

Cinderella took up her calligraphy wand and began sketching birds. The guinea fowl did not come out right, but she was sure that she could create wonderful birds with practice. She had an idea. Eggs were easy to draw! She drew an egg and labeled it a phoenix egg. The egg rolled out of the page and into her bedroom. I really can't be sitting on this, she thought, and kindly set the egg aside. I'll have to learn to actually draw birds. She began with a sparrow and was delighted to see the wonderful creature fly out of her pages to perch along the walls. She drew parakeets, parrots, and love birds. One of the love birds was missing an eye. Oops. She'll have to remember to draw it in next time. Then she drew birds that no one had ever seen before. She drew kingfisher birds with brilliant blue feathers, and green tropical birds with yellow markings. There were 48 gorgeous creatures in all. "My feathery friends," she addressed them, "You are now free."

Tea Cozies and Terabytes: People

She waved her wand in dramatic circles, but lost grip on the wand. The palace disappeared as the calligraphy pen left her hand and flew toward a miniature play tea set on the dresser. The pen crashed and clanked among the stoneware.

Cindy froze and heard a rustling across the hallway. The noise woke up her brother Darrell. She quickly slipped off her dress and put on her regular clothes: long blue pants and her brother's old grey shirt.

"Hey, Fatty Catty, why you up so early?" He was coming. Cindy dashed for the door to lock it. "Let me in!" shouted Darrell. Cindy heard the familiar clinkety clink clank of an Allen wrench snaking into the bedroom door locking mechanism. She grabbed the button lock on her side and said, "Go away. Leave me alone." She used both of her thumbs to push back against the Allen wrench.

Footsteps thudded away. She won the battle. He was gone, but after a moment of silence, footsteps thudded back for round two. Cindy grabbed the doorknob and dug in. Darrell fumbled on the floor outside. Cindy jumped back just as a twelve-inch blade came slicing across the floor, where her feet used to be. The door opened, and all the beautiful birds turn into bats.

"Happy birthday, fat face. Eleven years of flubbering your fat. How does it feel?" Each bat carried a new slap to her face from every direction. "How about some birthday punches?" Curling into a ball didn't help. The slapping bats continued.

Cindy shouted, "Stop. Please stop."

"Stop what?" he said. Five more slaps. Eight more.

"Stop slapping me!" Ten pinches from all directions. "Ouch!"

"I'm not slapping you." More pinching.

"Stop pinching me!" Now there were punches instead of pinches.

"It's your birthday. Don't you want your birthday punches?" Darrell asked menacingly.

Cindy couldn't see in the flurry of arms and bats. Her hands found the knife orphaned on the floor. She grabbed it and flung the blade into the blur of arms and bats.

Darrell screamed, "Ahhhrgh! You retard! I was only playing! I'm telling Mom!" He bolted, screaming, "Maahhm!" The knife clanked to the floor, leaving scars on the otherwise pristine blonde wood.

Cindy was left in the empty room with an open hand over the knife. The bats returned to their perches high up all around the perimeter of the room. They frowned at her like gargoyles frowning upon the sinners entering Notre Dame. Cindy counted 47 bats all along the walls. One bat was missing. She found it lying on the floor. It had turned back into a beautiful tropical bird, with iridescent soft blue feathers. She brought the creature into her hands and tried to keep it warm. It was no use. Darrell was unharmed, but the tiny innocent creature was gone forever. Cindy looked up at the gargoyles for help and sobbed.

Cindy and Darrell were both disciplined. Cindy had to stay in her room for thirty minutes and write, "I will not fight with my brother" fifty times. Darrell had to stay in his room for thirty minutes and write: "I will not take kitchen utensils without permission" fifty times. Mom thought this was just another squabble among siblings, and Cindy's birthday would not be cancelled.

Cindy got to work at her kid-sized drawing desk. She used scrap paper from the kitchen with advertisements on the other side and got out her beloved calligraphy pen. Darrel had broken the kid-size chair about a month ago, so Cindy had stacked up thirty books to sit on as she worked at the desk. The calligraphy pen skipped on the grain of the plywood surface as she wrote the first line. As soon as the period dotted the end, one of the bats flew out the window. With each line, another bat was gone, and Cindy felt the weight of their intense gaze diminish with each departure. As Cindy wrote, dutifully serving her sentence, she heard her brother's door creak open ahead of schedule.

"Mom?" called Darrell in a honey-sweet tenor voice.

"Yes, dear?" Mom responded.

"I'm really sorry I didn't ask you first about the kitchen knife. I just really wanted to get in and wish my little sister a happy birthday."

"I know you did, sweetie, but fair is fair. Get back in your room," she said firmly.

Darrell stalled, "I want to be a priest when I grow up. Can I pray for Cindy instead of writing lines?"

"That's very thoughtful of you, Honey," Mom cooed. "Yes, you can do that, instead. Still thirty minutes. Now, back to your room."

Cindy heard the door creak closed again. In another moment, she heard the familiar wumpf of Darrell's plastic toy box opening. Cindy took out another scrap piece of paper, this time with an ad from Goodwill on the back. The bats were half gone. At long last, the last two bats carried away the lifeless body of the azure kingfisher. Before fluttering away, they rested upon the windowsill and looked back at Cindy, "Your father will know about this," they threatened and flickered away.

Thirty minutes were up, but Cindy stayed in her room, practicing drawing with her calligraphy pen in her new notebook.

She drew dozens of individual beaks and feathers until the room was crawling with hungry bodiless beaks and swirling with feathers.

Mom walked in with Darrell, but they didn't seem to notice the storm of beaks and feathers. "Did you want to go to Greenville's Fun Land or Aladdin's Arcade for your birthday?" Mom asked. Cindy was a little confused. She had been talking about Greenville's Fun Land for the past week.

"Aladdin's Arcade!" Darrell shouted without invitation. "I want to go to Aladdin's. We were just at Greenville's two months ago."

"It's Cindy's birthday, and Cindy gets to choose," Mom said.

"Cindy, let's go to the arcade. It will be awesome. I'll show you all the cool games. Please, please, please." Darrell smiled and held her hand. He could be so charming. He held his hands up for a double high five. "Aladdin's! What do you say?"

Cindy hated arcades. Yet, the invitation was irresistible. She jumped to reach her brother's high five's and chimed, "Aladdin's it is."

"Darrell, make sure you stay with your sister, and

make sure she gets a chance to play."

Mom took Cindy and Darrell to Aladdin's Arcade. Mom had asked Cindy if she wanted to bring any of her friends. Cindy replied, "No. I asked them and they said they were all busy today. Amanda had to go to her cousin's birthday." It was true that Amanda was at her cousin's birthday, but in fact, Cindy had not asked anyone to come to her birthday party. Mom did not press the issue, and Darrell chimed in, "More fun for me!"

Following instructions, Darrell led Cindy through the arcade. "You don't wanna play Kangaroo, and you don't wanna play Popeye. Those games are lame. Asteroids is wicked. Pac Man and Space Invaders are long time faves. Everybody loves Donkey Kong. Let's get you started on Pac Man. The controls are pretty easy. Up goes up."

Cindy was actually going to play a game. Darrell inserted a coin and pressed "start." Cindy tilted her head way back to get a good view of the screen. "Hurry up," said Darrell, the ghost is going to eat you." Sure enough, Pac Man was quickly eaten up by a ghost. "You should try one more time." Another coin. Cindy lasted longer this time, collecting all the cherries and leveling up. "This one's harder," said Darrell. "You need to immediately go right."

"What is the point of playing if you don't get to figure that out on your own?" thought Cindy. She turned left and was immediately eaten by a ghost.

"Airhead," said Darrell. "Here, let me play one."

Cindy knew that was her last game. She watched patiently, admiring her brother's skill in eating the cherries and leveling up. She cautiously cheered him on as he advanced through each level. It kept peace to keep Darrell busy. The moments between levels were interspersed with positive exclamations, "Bodacious! Fantabulous! Wicked awesome!"

Watching was safer than playing, but it wasn't as interesting. Cindy thought about stealing away with her sketchbook. Darrell had all the coins. While Darrell was focused on mastering level 7, Cindy muttered, "I'm going to checked out the play set," and left.

Cindy thought that she might hate her brother, and that she might want to be like her brother. She recounted, impressed, "I died twice within two minutes, and Darrell has been playing for at least 20 minutes without dying once." "But I don't really like video games," she thought, "and I'm kind of a loser at them." She walked aimlessly around the play set, between swings and geometrical climbing shapes. She took a seat on a swing and leaned back to gain height. "Was Darrell bad?" She mostly liked Darrell when he was nice to her, but he could be really mean toward her, too. Cindy could not remember a day when she was not called a name or hit. "I'm sure there was at least one day," she thought, "but I don't remember one." Cindy leapt through the air to dismount the swing and landed on her feet. Mom always said that Darrell was just playing. It only looked like he was being mean, when he actually loved her. This explanation didn't make sense to Cindy, even though she would have wanted it to be true. She wanted Darrell to be happy, so she was glad she chose the arcade, even though Fun Land would have been more fun for herself. Fun Land had an indoor plastic play castle that was four stories high, and a multi-tiered slide running down from it. "This slide is just as good," thought Cindy, as she assessed the one-story tubular slide.

It was tougher to run up the slide than to climb the stairs and slide down, so Cindy ran up the slide. She almost ran out of steam at the top but flung herself forward and grabbed onto the floorboards. She kicked and pulled herself up to safety. Looking out from the slide tower, she could see Mom in line to order pizza and cake. Darrell was probably still playing Pac Man, or else he moved onto Donkey Kong or Mario Brothers.

Cindy hid in the slide tower and pulled her sketchbook and calligraphy pen out of her backpack.

Darrell had quietly climbed up the slide. It was much easier for him than it was for Cindy. "Hey, Birthday girl, it's time to stuff some pizza into your fat face."

"Again?" thought Cindy.

She continued to draw. She did not look up.

"Fat face, Mom wants us to eat the pizza now," Darrell insisted.

"Give me a minute," Cindy replied.

Darrell would not be ignored. "Now!" he shouted. He grabbed the sketchbook out from her hands, but it was a gift from Zeus. The sketchbook glowed red hot, then white, and Darrell threw it away from himself in utter terror. "You filthy fat witch!" he yelled. The sketchbook landed across the fence, in an area that was taped off.

"You lost my sketchbook!" cried Cindy. "You go get it now."

"Serves you right. I'm gonna tell Mom you threw it at me."

"You liar!"

"What you gonna do about it? Cry? Draw a picture of

yourself crying? Let me wipe those baby tears," he gushed lugubriously. He grabbed her face and squished her reddening cheeks in.

"Stop it," Cindy pleaded.

Surprisingly, Darrell stopped. "You better come now and get pizza," he ordered and left.

Cindy followed, without her notebook. She took one last glance at it. It landed open on the concrete. The last spread faced up, and Cindy smiled as she saw another sparrow emerge from the paper. It was missing a leg, but it still hopped about and smiled, full of life. Cindy wiped her tears and went to eat pizza.

Mom always ordered plain cheese and sausage pizza whenever they ate out, which was rare. After one slice of pizza, three vanilla cupcakes arrived. One of them had two candles in it. "Mommy, I'm eleven, not two," Cindy whined.

"Shut-up," Darrell retorted, "It makes an eleven, you see, stupid?"

"Honey," Mom tried to explain, "They only had cupcakes today, and two candles look much prettier on that cute little cupcake than eleven candles would." They sang "Happy Birthday," and Cindy wished that Darrell really would love her and be nice to her. As she inhaled a deep breath, Darrell blew out her candles.

Mom relit the candles, and Cindy blew them out quickly, possibly before the original wish could also be relit, but honestly, who knew if wishes worked anyway.

Late that night, a flashlight lit up the bedroom. Cindy collected her scrap paper, for lack of a sketchbook, and her calligraphy pen under the covers to continue drawing by flashlight. The scrap paper didn't work as well as the sketchbook. None of the wings she drew came to life, and finally the ink itself lightened to a thin grey line and was gone. No ink. No sketchbook. How stupid and pathetic to be drawing without ink or paper. She pressed the nib of the calligraphy pen into the side of her foot and traced a feather where this morning's knife could have landed. "I will draw myself some wings," she thought, as she traced a feather over and over again for lack of paper and ink. She traced beyond pain and stopped when the nib flowed red. The ink tasted like iron. Cindy fell asleep, with wings.

* * *

Eleven years later, Cindy could still trace the self-inflicted scar from her eleventh birthday. Self-harm was a learned habit. Cindy wondered whether or not the habit could be unlearned. That question seemed more important than correctly identifying where fantasy began and ended, or correctly remembering whether Darrel had used a twelve-inch chef's knife or a six-inch paring knife, or even correctly understanding whether there was malice in her mother's blindness or merely the apathy of having long ago accepted malevolence as normal within her own world. What mattered to Cindy was the simple question of whether or not a habit could be unlearned.

Meet the WordWeavers

Jennifer McMurrain

Editor-in-Chief - President

Having a great deal of wanderlust, Author Jennifer McMurrain traveled the countryside working odd jobs before giving into her muse and becoming a full time writer. She's been everything from a "Potty Princess" in the wilds of Yellowstone National Park to a Bear Researcher in the mountains of New Mexico. She has won numerous awards for her short stories and novels, including hitting #1 on the Amazon Best Seller list, in the paid market, with her debut novel, *Quail Crossings*. She has six full length novels, seven book collaboration, and ten novellas and short stories published. She lives in Bartlesville, Oklahoma with her family. You can find more information at www.jennifermcmurrain.com.

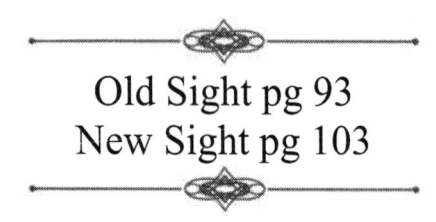

Old Sight pg 93
New Sight pg 103

www.jennifermcmurrain.com
www.annaslegacy.com
Facebook: https://www.facebook.com/pages/Author-Jennifer-McMurrain/351791824847958
Twitter: @Deepbluejc
Google+: Jennifer McMurrain
Tumblr: http://jennifermcmurrain.tumblr.com/
Instagram: http://instagram.com/jennifermcmurrain
Pinterest: http://www.pinterest.com/deepbluejc/
Goodreads: https://www.goodreads.com/JenniferMcMurrain
Amazon Author Page: Jennifer McMurrain

Marilyn Boone

Vice President

Marilyn is a former elementary school teacher who taught in every grade, from first to fifth. Inspired by faith and family, her first young adult novel, Heartstrings, won the juvenile published book category at the Oklahoma Writer's Federation annual contest in 2016. She has since added two more novels, Becoming Rose and Lillian's Locket, to this series of Legacy novels. Marilyn also enjoys writing poetry, essays and other fiction, and has had a story published in Chicken Soup for the Soul: Reboot Your Life. When not writing, she enjoys playing her hammered dulcimer, walking her dog, Emma, named after one of her favorite characters of course, and searching for great recipes.

Finding Thanks pg 4

www.marilynboone.com

Jayleen Mayes

Secretary

Jayleen S. Mayes is a lifelong "Potterhead" with a craving for all things magical, paranormal, and creepy. Jayleen does have a softer side when it comes to her writing, throwing in inspiration with real life magic. When she is not writing she enjoys being a foodie and drinking copious amounts of coffee. Jayleen also teaches English at Bartlesville High School.

Space Cowboy pg 66

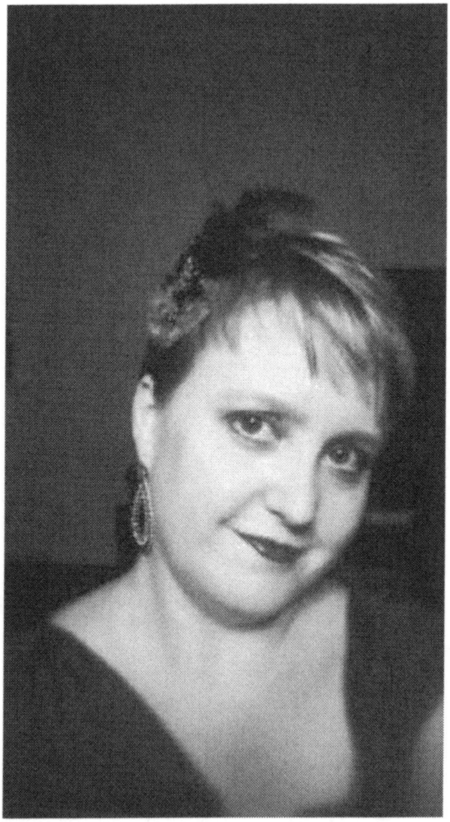

R. D. Sadok

Treasurer

R.D. "Rick" Sadok and his wife, Kristine, currently live in Bartlesville, Oklahoma. After retiring from his career as a chemical engineer, Mr. Sadok now pursues his first vocational love which is writing novels from a Christian world view. He invites you to visit his website at rdsadok.com for more information.

Frank's Five Hundred MPH Mouse pg 128
Awards Ceremony pg 144

https://rdsadok.com/

https://www.facebook.com/rick.sadok

Olive Swan

Public Relations

An incorrigible daydreamer since childhood, Olive Swan decided during a summer in college to write down some of the stories floating around in her head. Voila! A writing hobby was born. In 2010, she published her first novel, *New Creation: One Man's Six Day Transformation*, a contemporary, Christian romance.

Olive grew up in northern Illinois and recently moved to Oklahoma. She got involved in the vibrant writing scene in the northeastern part of the state. A project coordinator by day, in her free time she researches and writes both contemporary and historical fiction. She also blogs at her website, theoliveswan.com.

Olive's goal is two-fold, to tell stories of significance and to write with excellence. And if she's not doing that, there's a good chance, she's probably off daydreaming.

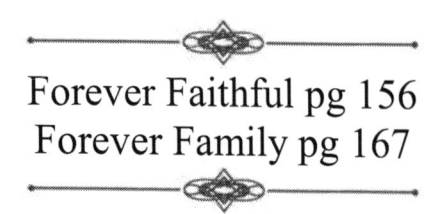

Forever Faithful pg 156
Forever Family pg 167

https://theoliveswan.com/

C. L. Collar

C. L. Collar is a down-to-earth country girl who has lived most of her life in small town America. She has a passion for laughter and a strong love of God and family. C. L. was introduced into the world of magic and poetry by her mother at a very young age through the book *Silver Pennies,* and fell in love with fanciful writing. She shares much of her work on her blogs. You can also friend her on Facebook. C. L. Collar currently has two books published, *The McCory Chronicles: Katie McCory and the Dagger of Truth* and *Finding Fey: A Book of Fairy Tales.* Both are available on Amazon. She presently lives in Darrouzett, Texas with her husband and a very extensive furry family.

When Snowflakes Fall pg 11

http://creationsmystique.blogspot.com/
http://mccorychronicles.blogspot.com/
Facebook: https://www.facebook.com/cathy.collar
Facebook: https://www.facebook.com/CLCollar
Amazon Author Page: C.L. Collar

Linda Derkez

Linda Derkez has been a writer since the second grade. She's the author of two poetry collections which includes *Jane Eyre and Other Poems Gathered from the Pages of the Classics* as well as several children's books, including the Manny the TV Watching Dog Series (written with Mike Derkez). Her children's story about bullying, *Henny the Brave Chicken*, won second place in her local 2016 Friends of the Library Creative Writing Competition. Additionally, she received an honorable mention in poetry for "Restless Heart" in the 2016 Oklahoma Writer's Federation Inc. contest. Linda contributed to *Seasons Remembered* and *Seasons of Life*, both WordWeaver anthologies.

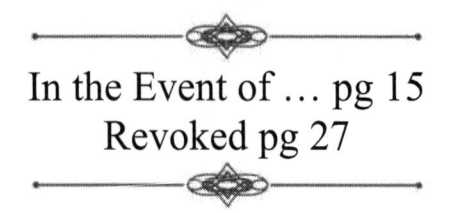

In the Event of … pg 15
Revoked pg 27

http://www.angelfire.com/stars4/kswiesner/linda.html
Amazon Author Page: Linda Derkez

Rita Durrett

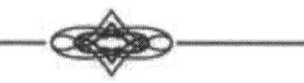

Rita Durrett is the author of four Young Adult and three Romantic Suspense novels, an award-winning Children's story, and dozens of short stories and novellas.

Over 40 years in the field of education have given Mrs. Durrett insight and knowledge about teenagers, their inner turmoil, and resilient nature. Her mid-west living and frequent cruise trips provide the perfect resource for suspense, adventure, and romance.

Rita shares her home in Elk City, Oklahoma with her mother. Her life is enriched by being mother to two sons and grandmother to six boys and one girl. She also has three grand-dogs that might lick an intruder to death, but she admits, wouldn't bite unless someone was getting between them and their food.

Friends Forever pg 39
Houdini pg 48

Tea Cozies and Terabytes: People

www.ritadurrett.com
Amazon Author Page: Rita Durrett

Meredith Fraser

Meredith Fraser creates stories for children and those children at heart. She is a member of the Society of Children's Book Writers and Illustrators and the Oklahoma Writer's Federation Inc. She received first place in the picture book category at the 2018 OWFI annual writing contest. Meredith taught first grade before becoming a mother of three and then a grandmother of three. She loves looking at this world through a child's eyes and creating a story from each experience. When she isn't writing or exploring nature with her grandchildren, Meredith is helping her husband with the 3,700-acre museum and wildlife preserve he manages. She lives in Oklahoma with her husband, a stray cat, and a rescue dog.

Butterfly Mims pg 52

Tea Cozies and Terabytes: People

Pepper Hume

Pepper Hume is an artist who deals in pictures and words, do not trust her with numbers. Being a refugee from the gypsy life of professional theatre design, she tends to think in four dimensions, often in reverse. Add compulsive people-watching and reading, and that's why she writes. She is really a nice, little old widow lady whose cat, a notoriously picky eater, recently gifted her with a headless dead squirrel on her birthday.

Rock Chalk Jayhawk KU pg 57
A Red Tri Aussie pg 66

Tea Cozies and Terabytes: People

e-mail: pepperh@dcworx.com

Glen Mason

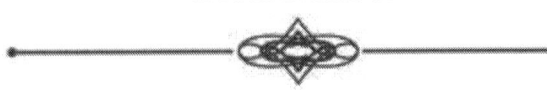

Glen was born, raised, and educated in rural Blackwell, Oklahoma; attended Phillips University in Enid, Oklahoma; graduated with a degree in chemistry; and served in the United States Navy. He married Sharon A. Reinking in 1968; together they raised a son and a daughter. In his career, he worked as a chemist, quality engineer, and safety manager for various companies located in Oklahoma, Montana, and Arkansas.

With a lifelong love for, and abiding interest in music, Glen takes guitar lessons and practices daily, and listens to a wide variety of musical styles. Recently retired, he plans to spend more time writing, practicing music, volunteering, and working in the yard and flower beds.

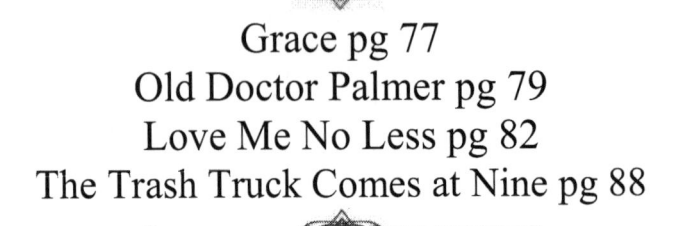

Grace pg 77
Old Doctor Palmer pg 79
Love Me No Less pg 82
The Trash Truck Comes at Nine pg 88

Tea Cozies and Terabytes: People

Cindy Molder

Cindy Molder is from Shelbyville, Tennessee, a small town outside of Nashville. She married her high school sweetheart Mark. They have two grown sons, a daughter in love, and twin grandsons. She and Mark have lived in Tennessee, Alabama, North Carolina, Florida, and Oklahoma. Cindy's travels around the southeast provide the back drop for most of her writing. A southerner through and through, she says she is a Tennessee girl living (and writing) in an Oklahoma world.

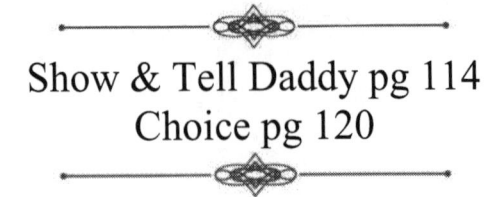

Show & Tell Daddy pg 114
Choice pg 120

http://cindymmolder.wordpress.com/
https://www.facebook.com/cindy.molder

Eloise Peacock

Eloise Peacock wrote and edited a newsletter for the Annapolis, Maryland area Amnesty International for nine years, and produced and copy-edited a newsletter for an international non-profit based in Washington D.C. for eleven years (SEARAC - Southeast Asia Resource Action Center). She studied genre fiction at UCLA, and fiction with Richard Peabody at St. Johns College and the Bethesda Writers Center. Eloise won third place for suspense/crime novel and second place for sci-fi short story at the Oklahoma Writers Federation, Inc. conference in 2015.

Wednesday Morning pg 124

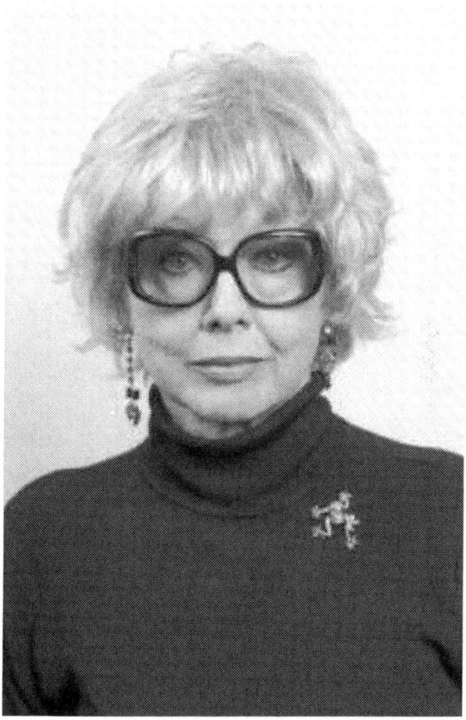

Antoinette Yvette Mousseau

Antoinette Yvette Mousseau was born in Quebec, Canada and grew up in Springfield, Missouri. Mousseau moved to Bartlesville, OK in 2010 and became a member of the Bartlesville Word Weavers in 2017.

Mousseau kept a journal as a child and cultivated a strong imagination. Her first works of creative writing were poetic songs about friendship, sunshine, puppies, and other objects of interest to eight-year-olds. Mousseau adores magic realism for the outlet it provides for the perpetual eight-year-old within, and for its ability to express complex emotional states. Aside from writing, Mousseau's other interests include chemistry and horticulture.

The Age of Silicon pg 185
The Age of Iron pg 191

Tea Cozies and Terabytes: People

Brandy Walker

Cover Designer

Brandy Walker, a self-professed lover of all arts, grew up in small town U.S.A. before finding her way to Albuquerque, New Mexico to study art in both the classroom and everyday life. Whenever possible, she and her three furry friends take road trips to fulfill her love of photography. She now owns her own graphic design studio, Sister Sparrow Graphic Design, in Colorado Springs, CO.

Tea Cozies and Terabytes: People

Facebook:
https://www.facebook.com/SisterSparrowDesign
www.sistersparrowgraphicdesign.com

The WordWeavers

All profits from the sale of this anthology will be used for the expenses of WordWeavers: handing out scholarships to writing conferences, educational speakers, and providing reading enjoyment to the community.

Made in the USA
Lexington, KY
24 February 2019